RECOMPENSE

A WORLD WAR II NOVEL

RUSS HAMACHEK

HARA
PUBLISHING GROUP

Published by
Hara Publishing
P.O. Box 19732
Seattle, WA 98109

Copyright ©2003 by
Russ Hamachek
All rights reserved

ISBN: 1-883697-62-X

Library of Congress Catalog Card Number:
2002113541

Manufactured in the United States
10 9 8 7 6 5 4 3 2

Also by Russ Hamachek:
Hot, Straight and True - An Anecdotal
View of PT boats in World War II

Editor: Vicki McCown
Cover Design: Scott Fisher
Book Design & Production: Scott and Shirley Fisher

Again —
To Margaret, aka "Muggsie,"
beloved wife, friend, and companion
lo these fifty-plus years

ACKNOWLEDGMENTS

Although the author is one of the "old men" of World War II's PT boat service, nothing in this text is autobiographical except indelible memories of PT operations in its New Guinea ambience. All events and characters are meant to be imaginary. Incidentally, for the uninitiated, since none exist in today's Navy, "PT" is an acronym for Patrol Torpedo—sometimes referred to as an MTB or Motor Torpedo Boat.

The personal focus of these recollections has been considerably embellished by the authoritarian contributions of my initial squadron commander and steadfast mentor Rear Admiral Barry K. Atkins USN (retired), the help and encouragement of friend and admired colleague Captain Hugh Robinson USN (retired), and since this tale prominently features a court-martial, a special reliance on the Naval legal expertise of Brigadier General James E. Herbold USMC (retired).

Above and beyond information regarding the infamous "Death March of Bataan" gleaned from numerous publications, a much more intimate portrayal was gained in conversation with former Marine Corps Corporal Robert R. Mitchell, who endured that damnable ordeal and subsequent imprisonment—to return to civilian life at the close of the war and succeed mightily in the somewhat less arduous world of banking.

Greatly helpful in gaining some insight and, hopefully, clarification in the cryptic vale of Australian idiomania is Aussie-turned-Yankee, fellow Arizona denizen Perce Judd.

Last, and far from least, are the colorful exchanges with other motor torpedo boat veterans in post-war reunions and the friendships still extant despite the accelerating erosions of time.

FOREWORD

"Clandestine" is the appropriate word for the Coastwatchers of World War II. Of necessity, their perilous and vital contributions to the final Allied success were intentionally given little publicity at the time — and strangely enough, remain undeservedly obscure to this day.

Residing in down-under Asia, geographically speaking, Australians and New Zealanders sometimes feel a bit isolated from what they consider "their Western world." Isolated yes, and somewhat lonely at times: particularly so in the pre-WWII era when they observed some of the Asians — chiefly the Japanese — arming, charting their nearby waters, and making no bones about their desire for what the Germans would term "lebensraum."

As a result, beginning in the early twenties, these "Downunders" set up a loose system of volunteer observers: government people, missionaries, planters — whoever knew a region or an island and was known in it — to watch for and report potential threats to the continental interests.

The earliest manifestation of the expansion-mindedness of the Japanese was their occupation of Manchuria in 1931, followed by the equally sanguinary assault on China itself. Even the United States was affected with the sinking of the *Panay* on December 12, 1937.

Shortly thereafter, the Japanese made their grandiose plans official with the establishment of what they euphemistically termed "The Greater East Asia Coprosperity Sphere." To augment the decision, they chose sides—cozying up to the Germans in 1940, and a short time later occupying French Indo-China.

With the outbreak of war in Europe, the Australians decided to formalize their Islands Coastwathching Service. Their navy put it in the hands of a one-time lieutenant commander-turned warden of the Wau Gold Fields of northern New Guinea named Eric Feldt. Working from his new headquarters in Townsville, in Queensland, Australia, he established a network of covert, radio-equipped informants throughout the entire umbrella of islands surmounting Australia and New Zealand: from Sumatra eastward through the rest of Indonesia, the New Guinea-New Britain area and, finally, the Solomon Islands. Information gathered was evaluated, consolidated and forwarded to their military and, later, that of the United States Pacific forces as well.

The United States took exception to these expansionist aspirations of the Japanese, suggesting they undo their aggressions and forgo any further incursions. While representatives of the two countries were ostensibly negotiating the matter in Washington, Tojo sent Yamamoto and his armada eastward across the Pacific to execute the catastrophic Pearl Harbor sneak attack of Sunday, December

7th, 1941—coordinated with the simultaneous December 8th Philippine assault on the western side of The Dateline.

With the resultant decimation of the United States Pacific fleet, unusual emphasis was given the PT boat program as a hastily available deterrent to further enemy aggression while the larger and more traditional capital ship fleet was being repaired and expanded. Relevence is given the gratifying result with their part in the legend that follows.

Russ Hamachek

1

Motor torpedo boat, PT 150, glided stealthily northward toward the enemy-held New Guinea shore. Its three roaring Packard V-12 Supermarines had been throttled back and muffled four miles out at sea as it left the 120 boat—its companion for the night. Only a purling whisper presaged the 4000-plus explosive horsepower in its engine room. General Quarters had been sounded, guns loaded with firing mechanisms at the ready and all hands admonished to maintain extreme silence, along with the most essential activity of all: utmost, unwavering vigilance.

The two officers were on the steel-encircled bridge: Executive Officer Mike Stringer at the wheel. Boat Captain Andy McCloud checking the readiness of the personnel. All guns were properly manned: 37-millimeter on the bow, a bit aft and to port; a 20-millimeter Oerlikon; the twin 50-caliber machine guns in their turrets—one abutting the starboard side of the bridge, the other on the after port side of the day room canopy; and finally, largest of all: the 40-millimeter Bofors cannon just forward of depth charges and smoke generator at the stern.

As predicted, the night was clear, moonless and black, the sea relatively calm—increasingly so as the boats left the main body of New Guinea's Solomon Sea and entered the sheltered lee of the Huon Gulf near the Japanese-occupied city of Lae.

Continuing to look aft, McCloud nodded approvingly at the translucent evidence of fine boat handling: an arrow-straight wake seemingly etched into the eighty-odd nautical miles back over the horizon toward the motor torpedo boat Advanced Base at Morobe—site of the meeting that had delineated the rationale and plan for the operation now underway.

— —

He recalled Squadron Commander Gordon Winters' introduction of the stranger, the tousled, wind-blown Australian now at his side.

"McCloud, meet Jim Jollymore—your passenger for the night. And, Jim, this is Andy McCloud, skipper of PT 150." The boat captain put out his hand. "Pleased to meet you, Jim."

"Pleasure's mine, by jingo," smiled the visitor.

He seemed mild-mannered, but then, mused McCloud, judging by that hawked nose and determined chin, he was probably more rugged than he seemed at first glance.

The squadron commander continued. "Andy, I want you to put Jim ashore as surreptitiously as possible at a spot he will designate near Lae. And, although it's not easy to believe, he's going ashore *alone!*"

"Alone? But, Commander, the Japs—!"

"Yes, I know, Andy. It's firm Japanese territory at the moment. You might believe both Jim and I are dealing from a short deck—and I could hardly blame you. But when you hear the entire plan and it's rationale, I believe you'll agree with the entire strategy, it's importance, and the necessity for him to go ashore surreptitiously and alone."

"This character—and I think I use the term advisedly— is what is called a 'coastwatcher.' You know about them, don't you, McCloud?"

Glancing at the Australian, then back to the commander, McCloud pursed his lips in a half smile. "I sure do, Commander, but not first hand. I'm well aware of the intelligence we gain from them, and it's value, but unlike some of the fellows, I haven't had any experience landing or picking them up. The one thing I do know is that I'd rather do *that* than be one of them!" With the remark, Jollymore's face broke into an appreciative grin.

"I understand, Andy," said Commander Winters, "and agree with you completely. And along that line, I must warn you that what you're about to hear and do tonight is confidential in the extreme. What fellows like Jim do is highly vital to our war effort and some awfully valuable lives are at stake. Knowing you and your crew, I'm sure you'll do an effective job tonight, but by all means, keep it to yourselves—before, during, and ever-after. Caution the entire crew: 'Mum's the word. Understand?"

"Yes, Sir, I understand—and, of course, we'll comply. But, Commander, are you implying we'll be running alone?"

"Oh no, nothing like that. Jack Longacre and his 120 boat is scheduled to be with you and—oh oh—you're right. I dropped the ball on that one." He glanced at the coastwatcher and smirked. "First time I've ever been wrong, you understand!" He called, "Childers!" and instantaneously, his yeoman appeared from a back room, springing to attention.

"Yes, Sir, Commander?"

"Childers, run down to the dock and ask Lieutenant Longacre to come right up."

"Aye aye, Sir," said the yeoman, and off he bounded, down the steps and down the trail, the screened door banging behind him.

"Now," continued Winters, turning to Jollymore, "while we're waiting for Longacre, how about wetting our lips? What would you like, Jim?"

"That's right on, mate," said the coastwatcher brushing back his errant cowlick. "I'm dry as a pommy's towel. A tinny would start the day nicely, thank you."

The commander wrinkled an eye in bewilderment. "A pommy's towel? What's a 'pommy'?"

Jollymore returned the squint. "You're serious? You don't know?"

"That's right, I don't know—never heard of a 'pommy.'"

"Why, a Britisher of course."

"And why a Britisher?"

The Aussie's lip curled in a faint smile. "Well, you see. Commander, they—our Limey friends—are supposedly not famous for frequent bathing."

"Worse than the Germans?"

"Oh Lord, no—nothing like that, but compared to us tidy chaps—you Yanks included, of course—bad enough."

Gordon Winters smiled. "And a 'tinny' I suppose is a can of...a can of..."

"You guessed it, mate. A coldie—slops—suds. You know—a beer."

The squadron commander glanced at McCloud, then turned back to Jollymore and shook his head morosely. "I'm afraid we have to disappoint you, Jim. This is a United States command—no beer, no suds, no slops, no grog. How about a lemonade or a mug of coffee?" "A lemonade!" chortled Jollymore. "By cripes, I forgot you Septics have the world's only goody-goody navy. If you can't rort the system, sure, mate—I'll take that mug of java." "Hold on, old boy," said Winters. "You're way beyond me again. First, what's a 'Septic'? Doesn't sound exactly complimentary to me." "A Septic?" Jollymore grinned. "No need to be uptight, mate. Sounds bad, but it isn't. 'Yank' rhymes with 'septic tank,' so that's just sort of a nickname." Commander Winters scratched his head. "Oh, I see...I think. And 'rort the system'?" "Why, twist the rules, of course." The Commander laughed, turning to the boat captain. "I guess, Andy, the problem is ours. We just don't understand the King's English."

The exchange and the wait for Jack Longacre gave McCloud an opportunity to assess his surroundings. While the buildings below—the shops and hospital—were mostly steel quonset huts painted to blend in with the jungle, that wouldn't do at all for the commanding officer's hut here on it's hilltop. It was much too conspicuous a locale for that—especially with an occasional nighttime visit from "Wash Machine Charlie" searching for a target for its bombs in order to cripple the PT's that plagued their reinforcement efforts at Lae and Salamaua.

This building was different. Despite its steel deck and underlying roof structure, the exterior consisted of woven palm fronds—just another native hut to all outward appearances.

And now, here inside the hut, was this unique visiting personality: Coastwatcher Jim Jollymore.

Imagine, thought McCloud, a fellow volunteering to spend time in the immediate neighborhood of the enemy— close enough to espy, study, and report his actions via radio. That should require a giant of a man, but physically, this fellow isn't large at all. On the contrary, his slight build doesn't appear particularly rugged, but in this case, looks must be deceiving. Under that slight physique, there must be one tough and determined hombre.

Lieutenant Commander Winters looked up from the coffee he was pouring.

"Ah, here we are—welcome, Jack. Jim, this is Lieutenant Jack Longacre, captain of the 120 boat that will be accompanying you tonight; and Jack, this is Jim Jollymore, the coastwatcher you'll be landing near Lae." The two shook hands.

The squadron commander continued. "You know, Jim, everything we've discussed about the Nips and their ambitious plans spells trouble for your country—and except for the Coral Sea fracas, they might have their sandals on your shores right now."

Jollymore nodded. "That's about the full two-bob. I know what you mean, Commander, and you're right. The good guts is that we feel a tad better about it now. But, by cripes, it isn't over yet...no, not by a long shot. Knowing those Nips, s'treuth is despite all the room we have on that big island continent of ours, most of us squat down in the southeast corner of it. And when those yobbos began scrounging for even more scrub in the Western

Pacific, it became a bloody uncomfortable situation—and not just for the Top Enders."

"Excuse me, Jim," broke in Winters, "what's a 'Top Ender'?"

"Why, the blokes in the Northern Territory and Queensland, Commander—but they're not alone. It's true of the lot of us. And that's the straight up and down."

All three Americans nodded sympathetically.

"This fellow in charge of your Coastwatching System," asked Winters, "what sort of chap is he?"

"Oh, Eric Feldt? He's a tall poppie. Believe me, mates, they picked the right man in his case. He's doing a bonzer job."

The squadron commander nodded and smiled. "Yes, from all I've heard that's right on—as long as he surrounds himself with fellows like you, that is."

He turned to his two boat captains. "Andy, Jack, can you imagine the guts it takes to sneak in, set up camp, then sit alone in the middle of a Jap-infested island, watching what they—the Nips—are up to, then broadcasting what he sees, knowing full well *they're* listening in and manning a few radio direction finders to pinpoint his location—and eliminate it!"

Jollymore's raised hand stopped him. "Go on, Commander, it's not as bad as all that. We keep our messages brief as possible. And don't forget, most of us have knocked around the country we're assigned to, know the locals and their lingo or Eric wouldn't send us into it. And look who's talking! You're not exactly Nervous Nellies yourselves!"

"Excuse me, Jim, but I think you're making light of it. And incidentally, this turn of the conversation reminds me of the time I was engaged in an argument with a submarine skipper over who had the most dangerous assignment.

"I maintained that anyone who volunteered to go underwater in one of those metal tubes has holes in his head. He retaliated by saying anyone who ran around in what he termed 'a plywood runabout looking for battleships' had to be balmy. Finally he settled the dispute by slamming the table with his beer mug and bellowing: 'I've had enough of this crap!

"I want you to know we can do everything you can do—and one thing more. When I asked what that might be, he said: 'When we go under water, we fully expect to come up again!' And, like that sub skipper, I think you're making light of what you do. For example, Jim: isn't it true you change your personnel frequently?"

"Aye, Commander—that's right on."

"And why is that?"

"Oh—a number of reasons. There's disease: malaria, dengue, blackwater fever—things like that. But chiefly, there's what some chaps refer to as 'the spell of the tropics'. Hah!-spell of the tropics my arse. Sounds romantic, doesn't it? But s'treuth is, that's a touristy term—refers to a temporary stop-over. Actually, if you stay too long, it does get to you—turns you into an imbo.'

"That's an imbecile?"

"Strike me pink Commander: you're beginning to understand classic Australian! But, seriously, the good guts is that nobody but the bushies can spend too much time out there without going a bit island happy—knocked up —'troppo' we call it. We all have to get back down to the mob scene now and then: get caught up in the traffic mess, put down a few frosties, pat a skimpy's bottom...you know, the sort of thing called 'civilization.'"

Winters grinned in turn. "Sure, Jim, that's all perfectly logical. But how about the Japs? You do lose personnel to them occasionally, don't you?"

"Aye again. It has happened and most likely will again. They—the Nips—aren't the greatest fans of our work you know. And believe me, mates, that's fair dinkum in spades."

"I can imagine," said Winters. "Now, tell Andy and Jack why you're going ashore near Lae."

"It's because Jerry Donegal—the chap we have stationed there—has stopped broadcasting for some reason. I'm going in and take an optic."

Jack Longacre broke in. "Excuse me, Jim, but what's an 'optic'?"

"Oh come now. Lieutenant Have a quickie—look around to find out why."

Gordon Winters shook his head. "Jim, you'll have to excuse me again, but it seems you've just done a first class job of proving my point: You fellows are an amazingly hardy group. Now, let's suppose you find his radio has broken down. Then, what will you do?"

"Fix the bloody squaller."

"Fix it?"

"Sure, mate," said Jollymore, tapping his head, "my noggin's into that."

"I understand," said the commander, "but what if something's blown out?"

"Oh I'm packing quite a bit of stuff—the parts most apt to 'blow out,' as you so quaintly put it."

"But, Jim, what if the radio is okay, but Donegal isn't?"

"In that case, I'll just have to hang my skivvies on his line."

Winters shook his head again. "Just like that, Jim, you'll hang...take his place!"

"Righto, mate. We just can't have any interruption in our knowledge of what goes on at Lae."

"But," interjected Jack Longacre, "what if both are fubar—the radio *and* your predecessor?"

"Fubar?" grimaced Jollymore. "Now I'm the imbo. What's 'fubar'?"

Longacre glanced at the squadron commander, receiving a nod and smile in reply. "Fubar—why, that's 'fucked up beyond all repair.'"

Jollymore laughed. " 'Fubar'—great word that. I can use it to help color my lingo. But, to answer your question, mate: If Eric Feldt doesn't hear from me in five days, you chaps will be asked to meet me again—same time, same spot."

Andy McCloud raised a hand. "Why go through all that waste of valuable time, Jim? Why not take another radio in to begin with?"

"Good question...but the answer is that it's not as easy as it sounds. These teleradios we use—with all their storage batteries, generator, and fuel—its a heap of gear. It takes about a dozen bushies to tote it all in—and since we don't know if the transmitter and receiver are both broken down, we have no way of knowing if Jerry knows I'm coming, or if Jerry himself is okay. No, it's best I take that optic—'get the lay of the land,' as you Yanks say. Then, if it's necessary, we'll have to ask you to bring the stuff I'm not taking in, and I and a group of my bush friends will meet you."

"Your bush friends?"

"Oh yes, I was a cocky."

"A cocky?"

"Go on, Commander—now you do disappoint me. A 'cocky' in flawless English is a small landholder. I was a cokie cocky."

"That's a coconut grower?"

"Well, starve the birdies, Commander—all is not lost! Your English is improving enormously!"

Gordon Winters grinned. "Thank you, Jim—that's high praise. Now, tell us. Where was that cokie cockie of yours?"

"As you might guess, right up near where Donegal is—in the neighborhood of Lae."

"And what happened to it?"

"The Japs moved in and sent me skeedaddling. But, to get to the point, we got along first rate."

"What! You and the Japs?"

"Hell's bells—no! The bushies, Commander."

"But Jim," commented Andy McCloud, "what if the Japs are their buddies now. Then, what will you do?"

"Oh, I'll just have to take that as it comes. However, I doubt if that's the way it is now. Knowing the Nips, if the usual pattern holds true that won't be the case. Their shenanigans in the past haven't earned them any gold stars with the bushies except where they—the Nips—have become so entrenched the bushies begin to think they're going to be there forever."

The squadron commander rubbed his chin. "If that's the criterion, this could be an example of it. After all, they've been at Lae for quite a spell." Just then, the light faded perceptibly, the fronds—top and sides—rustled, the entire hut seemed to vibrate. Looking about, he commented, "Looks like a front is coming through—you might have a little sea keeping you company tonight."

11

"S'all right. Commander, I enjoy a bit of a stir. But about those bushies at Lae, you're right. The Nips have been there for quite a spell. Still, I doubt if it's changed the bushies in this case. Your flyboys—with your help that is—have been giving those Nips some bad times lately. With them crawling in and out of their slit trenches all day, and you chaps raising hell with supply lines all night—plus the pressure our combined forces are putting on up the line at Dreger and Finschhafen—no, I doubt if the bushies think the buggers have the bloody war all wrapped up."

"All right, Jim," said Winters, "that takes care of the general plan for tonight's work. Now, you, Andy, and Jack can get together on the details." He turned to his boat captains. "And gentlemen, take good care of our new friend here. We certainly can agree that what these fellows do is enormously important to the overall war effort—to say very little of how vital it is to us. You understand, don't you?"

"Yes, Sir, we certainly do," said McCloud.

Jack Longacre nodded. "I'll drink to that."

Jollymore grinned. "With what—lemonade or coffee?"

— —

The boat captains and their passenger for the night strolled down the winding path to the boat dock where a PT which had patrolled the night before was fueling, then downstream under the swaying palms and their accompanying camouflage until they arrived at the 150 boat.

Jollymore paused, examining the 80-foot Elco with its crew readying it for the night's activities. Guns, torpedoes, depth charges, smoke generator, radio, and radar were all being checked, and food, ammunition, and other expendables carried aboard and stowed.

"What a great looking boat! Looks fast just sitting here. It is, isn't it?"

"Yes, sure is," replied McCloud, obvious pride in his voice, "when everything's in great shape. With her bottom squeaky clean—the boat's that is," he grinned, "and engines purring properly, she'll do 42 knots—about 48 miles an hour—with a war load, that is." The boat captain caressed the hull. "She's a good one all right. Runs great, especially when it's necessary...when she's scared, that is."

"Is it true they're made of plywood?" asked Jollymore. "Doesn't look like it."

"No," replied McCloud, "that's just an old wives' tale. Actually there are two half-inch strakes of mahogany over the frame with airplane cloth glued in between—then the whole thing is held together with a million copper nails and screws. Sounds fragile, I know, but actually, the resultant hull is flexible, but tough. It'll take more pounding than the crew can."

Jollymore pointed up at the boat's name emblazoned under the squadron insignia on the side of the cockpit. "Now, that's fair dinkum: *Miss Sing You*—I like that." He laughed. "Reminds me of a willowy sheila I bumped into in Townsville—and would like to rub up against again."

McCloud grinned. "Yes, you and all the rest of us: a wife, a girl, or just girls in general. You see, Jim, we had a contest to name the boat and when Mike Stringer—our executive officer—came up with this one, the game was over. And, speak of the devil," he pointed back down the path, "here's the author of the name now."

McCloud waved and called, "Hey, Mike, come on over. I'd like to introduce Jim Jollymore." The Australian and the executive officer shook hands. "Jim's a coastwatcher you're going to see a lot of tonight."

Jollymore looked up at the tall, lanky executive officer, then returned his gaze to the boat captain and grinned. "Well, blow me down! The tall one is the number two man and the short one—my size—is number one. How come, mates?"

Andy McCloud grinned. "Well, you see, Jim, in our Navy we go by brains—not height."

"And whose mother gave birth first," laughed Stringer.

"Speaking of oddities," said Stringer, "that name of yours—'Jollymore'—that's unique."

"Unique?" replied Jollymore. "How so?"

"Well," smirked Stringer, "justify it. Say something funny."

"Oh, come now," replied Jollymore, "you're just *stringing* me along."

Andy McCloud intervened. "Okay, you two. I can see you are destined to be great friends—you've already reached a draw.

"And now, if you characters will join Jack and me in the chart house, we can get down to a bit of strategizing." He turned to his executive officer. "You see. Mike—seriously now—we, with Jim here, have some important planning to do before this assignment gets underway."

2

The evening sun cast shadows causing a further enhancement of the green-and-black hull camouflage of the two PT's scheduled for the night's activities. Simultaneously, the engines of the 150 boat exploded into life, followed by those of the 120. Underwater exhausts were actuated, dropping the resonating roar to a burbling purr.

Lines were thrown, and with *Miss Sing You* in the lead, the boats pulled away from the bank to begin their winding trek down the inlet. With dusk closing in, they idled their way across the bay and, in consideration of the prevailing low stage of the tide, carefully threaded their way through the knife-like protrusions of the outer reefs.

Mufflers were bypassed and throttles advanced, pushing the boats up onto a 30-knot planing attitude for the run across the westward arm of the Solomon Sea toward their landfall of the night. As Squadron Commander Winters had predicted, a gusty wind was whipping the sea into a five- or six-foot chop—a gut-wrenching condition for the crews of the relatively flat-bottomed motor torpedo boats.

Glancing over at their guest of the night who was sharing the cockpit with the two boat officers, Andy McCloud thought he noticed an increasing pallor developing as the boat slammed its way from wave to wave.

"Sorry about the wild ride, Jim, but with the timetable you gave us, it can't be helped." He grinned. "But the bright side is that it'll only be a couple of hours before things begin to calm down."

"S'all right, mate," said Jollymore through clenched teeth, "I'll make it, by gum. And I'm glad you told me about how tough these boats are—I'd hate to swim in this mess."

True to his resolve, the plucky Australian succeeded in hanging on to his last meal during the torturous run up the coast, then to his relief, into the assuaging calm of the Huon Gulf. With Salamaua's peninsula to port, and Mike Stringer at the helm, Andy McCloud and Jim Jollymore stepped down to confer in the chartroom below. To Jollymore's momentary consternation, the light therein was dim and red in hue in order to attenuate the night blindness they were bound to experience when they returned to the darkness of the moonless night above.

Picking up a pencil, the boat captain pin-pointed a spot on the chart. "Here, Jim, if you can see in this light, this is where you want to go, isn't it?"

Jollymore peered at the chart, then looked askance. "In general, yes—but it just doesn't look quite right. Something's mucked up."

"I'm not surprised," said McCloud. "Look at the date on the chart issued to us. It's based on the surveys of d'Entrecastroux and Flinders in the late eighteenth

16

century! It's the best we have, but I agree it isn't much. We well know that, on this chart, Lae itself is several miles out of position.

"We learned that the hard way one foggy night when we tried to dead reckon ourselves to a position just outside of it in order to waylay a Nip submarine your Mister Donegal had reported in the harbor. Suddenly, we came out of the overcast to find ourselves knocking on their docks! Even worse, we weren't the only ones surprised. The Nips noticed it too, and getting out of there we damned near had our ass blown off. That, by God, was one of the nights we learned that *Miss Sing You* runs best when she's scared!"

Jollymore grinned. "Should've asked the Nips for a newer chart while you were there. Like I said this morning, with all the snooping they've been doing around here in late years, their maps must be up to snuff.'

"I'm sure you're right, Jim, and sooner or later, our Navy will get their hands on them and bring us up to date. But, as a substitute, take a look at this radar. Move it over. Sparks," said McCloud to the radio-radar operator. "Give our friend a view of the coast ahead."

The radar operator shifted the scope a bit. "Here you are, Sir."

Jollymore studied the scope, then shook his head.

"This helps, but I'm new at this radar business. I wish we had something I'm more familiar with."

"Try this, Jim," said McCloud, unrolling a strip photograph across the chart table and weighting the ends. "To do our job of intercepting the barge traffic effectively, we have to cozy up to the reefs, so we had the Air Force make us these strip photos. Take a look—perhaps they'll help."

17

The Australian studied them carefully. Finally he pointed. "Aye, mate, this is more like it. Here now—that's the place I want to go to."

McCloud leaned over to scan the photo. "Mmm—looks like we're lucking out. These air views give us a pretty fair look at the reefs, and the place you want to land seems clear. Okay, Jim, with that in mind, let's go topside and take a gander—you know—an 'optic.'"

After a few minutes on the bridge to allow their vision to adjust to the blackness, they looked shoreward.

Jollymore accepted a pair of seven by fifty power binoculars and studied the looming cliffs ahead. "There, Andy—over to the right a bit—where the ridge of that hill meets the strand...where the beach juts out. That's the spot I want."

"Swing her about ten degrees to starboard, Mike," said McCloud to Stringer. "Now, it's coming on. There—right on. Steady as she goes."

He picked up the microphone. "Easy Dog: This is where we'll be leaving you. See you when our job is done."

"Roger—and good luck" came the reply.

"Okay, Mike, mufflers on and, as we near the shore, take it down to an idle."

Some time later, with the cliffs looming ever-larger, McCloud ordered, "Now, Mike, drop to one engine."

"Aye aye, Andy." The executive officer signaled the engine room, putting the port and starboard engines in neutral and idling in on the center engine alone, which reduced the boat's forward speed markedly.

As they neared the shoreline, Jollymore said, "Andy, don't you think it's time for me to give it a go on my raft?"

The boat captain shook his head. "No, Jim let's see if we can do better than that. Remember the air photo we just looked at in the chartroom? You remember, it didn't show any reefs. Now look ahead. That cliff coming down to the shore seems to confirm it—promising enough water for us to creep in to that sand beach. We've a shallow draft—only draw a bit over six feet to the bottom of the screws. If we can put you right on the beach, it will save time—and be a lot safer for you."

"Ooright, mate," grinned Jollymore. "A bonzer thought...it has my vote."

McCloud nodded, then turned to the quartermaster manning the twin 50 caliber machine guns in the adjacent forward turret. "Barbell, come out of there and take your leadline position on the bow. When I signal, start the soundings, but don't sing out...just keep silent and wave us in if all seems okay. Got it?"

"Aye aye, Sir—got it."

McCloud touched his executive officer on the arm. "Mike, I'll take the helm. You take the working party and Jim forward and prepare to put him ashore."

A few moments later, McCloud signaled the waiting quartermaster, and Barbell, now on the starboard bow, threw the leadline, examined the result, and finding a favorable reading, motioned toward the shore. McCloud nodded and the PT eased forward. The leadline was thrown repeatedly and favorable results continued to be read.

Miss Sing You neared the beach, and as the remaining operating engine was put in neutral, the boat coasted to a near stop, then nuzzled the sand. A relieved McCloud spread his hands palms down as a signal to Stringer's group on the forecastle, then pointed ahead.

Jollymore's rubber raft was lowered to the strand, followed by a Jacob's ladder. Barbell and Jollymore swung over the side and down. Supplies were lined down into the raft and secured. Then, with Barbell's help, Jollymore dragged the raft up the beach and around behind the mangroves lining the foot of the cliff. Barbell returned and clambered aboard, pulling the Jacob's ladder after him. Shortly thereafter, a mangrove branch moved upwards and Jollymore reappeared with a rugged-looking native at his side. The native was obviously pleased—smiling and colorful with fuzzy hair, loin cloth amidships, and machete in hand. The coastwatcher grinned, doffing his hat in farewell. On the boat, both officers saluted.

"Good Lord," murmured Andy McCloud, "there is true grit personified!"

"Man oh man," breathed Stringer in turn, "I'll second that...and, you know, Andy, since that big native was there to meet him, it must mean that although the transmitter might be shot, the receiver is okay."

"By God, you're right, Mike."

McCloud signaled the engine room: "All engines astern." Then, with a nudge of the throttles, the resultant propeller backwash surged shoreward and *Miss Sing You* slid off the beach, backed into deeper water, came about, then headed for the open sea.

A half an hour and four nautical miles later, the 150 came alongside its companion 120 boat. Andy McCloud picked up the megaphone.

"Mission accomplished, Jack. Now, the night is young. Let's cruise up the shore and see if we can stir up some trouble."

"Roger, Andy," came the reply. "We're all for that. It's been boring as hell out here. Lead on."

3

Mufflers came off, and with the 120 boat following in seaward echelon, the 150 angled toward the reef-lined coast, proceeding in the direction of Vitiaz Strait which separates New Guinea from the neighboring Japanese-held island of New Britain.

The last time the Japanese attempted to reinforce beleaguered Lae via capital ships, the sixteen-ship convoy encountered the US Army Air Force, with some PT assistance in the Battle of the Bismarck Sea, culminating in the complete loss of all troop-carrying ships.

Since that calamity, the Japanese resorted to barges carrying armed troops and supplies surreptitiously operating as close to the coasts as possible. The Allied response was to chiefly rely on the shallow-draft, heavily-armed PT's to intercept and, if possible, destroy the barges.

Despite the fact that the newly installed radar in the 150 was operating, officers and lookouts in both boats focused their binoculars in a continual sweep of sea and coastline. With no moon, the mantle of stars was breathtakingly brilliant—a glistening panoply sweeping downward, culminating in Crux, the Southern Cross, re-splendent ruler of the horizon to starboard.

All proceeded without incident until a distraught-appearing older sailor—lead Motor Machinist Murphy, known as "Pappy" to the rest of the crew—appeared at the 150's bridge.

"Skipper, Sir, I think we've got a problem!"

"Murphy, what in the world are you doing up here! What's the problem?"

"It's Markowski, Sir. He's supposed to be in the engine room with me, but he isn't. He hasn't showed!"

"What do you mean 'he hasn't showed?' Since when?"

"Since we left that beach back there, and Skipper, I'm damned worried!"

"You mean you've been alone in the engine room—and there's *nobody* down there now?"

"Yes, Sir—that's right. I thought he'd show up at any time, but he hasn't. The kid's a no-show, and I thought you ought to know about it."

McCloud nudged his executive officer. "Did you hear that, Mike?"

"I sure did, Andy. And it doesn't make any sense!"

McCloud turned back to the motormac. "Okay, Murphy, get back to the engine room. We'll take it from here."

He called the quartermaster over and explained the situation. "Barbell, I want you to canvass the boat and crew." He smirked. "You'll probably find Markowski in the head."

Barbell began his search by peering down the hatch into the lazarette—the after-compartment of the boat chiefly devoted to exhausts, mufflers, and rudder equipment. An improbable place to find a missing man, thought Barbell, but what the hell, by "canvass" the old man must want me to be thorough, so I will.

Descending down the ladder into the mechanical clamor of the engine room, Barbell observed Pappy back on his seat aboard the starboard engine, but otherwise alone as reported. Next, he climbed up and forward into the day room that canopied the fuel tanks with their 3000 gallons of 100-octane fuel capacity. Then, it was down into the chartroom.

"Hey, Sparks," he called to the radio-radarman, "by any chance have you seen Markowski since we got underway from that beachhead?"

Sparks turned from his scrutiny of the radar scope. "Markowski? Up here? Hell no!"

Continuing his quest, Barbell swung down the ladder into "Officer's Country" below. Although he figured it another waste of time, in the continued interest of thoroughness he worked his way through the executive officer's cabin, the adjoining head, then the captain's cabin—all to no avail.

Next came a glance at the officer's booth-sized "wardroom," the galley, and through it to the crew's quarters forward. Seeing no sign of life, but recalling the skipper's parting comment, he checked the crew's head and, as an exaggerated but consummate measure, peered into the chain locker in the forepeak.

Emerging from the forecastle hatch, he returned to the bridge. "Skipper, I'm afraid Pappy's right. I've checked everything but the bilges. Nobody's seen him. Sir, he's simply not aboard this boat!"

Andy McCloud picked up the microphone. "Easy Dog: Believe it or not, we've lost a man—must have gone overboard. Let's come about and retrace our course. Have your men keep a sharp eye out for him, as we'll be doing."

The two boats came about and cruised slowly back up the coastline with all topside hands searching the surrounding sea for their missing comrade.

Finally, as they reached their original position off Jollymore's departure point, Andy McCloud signalled all engines into neutral. The 150 slowed, then stopped, and the 120 boat slid close alongside.

McCloud picked up his megaphone. "Jack: We're going to go back into the beach. I suggest you just search around out here until we return. And by all means, give us a call if you have any luck."

"Roger, wilco," came the answer, "and the same to you, Andy."

Resetting its mufflers so as not to alert the enemy to the importance of the area, the 150 idled in toward their former landfall, all hands continuing their scrutiny of the surroundings.

When within an effective viewing distance of the former beachhead, McCloud said, "Let's lay to for a bit, Mike—just in case Markowski made it to the beach and is hoping we'll show up."

After a brief, but disappointing spell, McCloud said, "Guess it's a no-go and no-show, Mike. Let's idle back out to the 120, continuing the search on the way. We just have to find the poor guy!"

Despite their thoroughness, the search proved worthless and, with dawn imminent, the two boats were again taken up to a thirty-knot cruising speed—pounding their way toward their Morobe base.

With the first blush of light accenting the eastern horizon, *Miss Sing You* began the precarious threading through the maze of reefs shielding the harbor entrance. Andy McCloud was at the wheel when the radio came to life with a warning from the 120 boat.

"Andy...Andy...something doesn't look right!" Simultaneously, a severe shock ran through the 150, followed by pronounced and severe vibration.

"Damn!" said McCloud, signalling the engine room to put the engines in neutral, then shut down. "What else can go wrong? I goofed. There goes at least one of the screws!"

"Well, look at it this way, Andy," said Mike Stringer. "It could have been worse."

"What do you mean, 'it could have been worse?'"

The executive officer glanced sidelong at his skipper. "It could have been me at the wheel!"

"Shit," began the growl from the boat captain, but his scowl melted into a grudging grin. "I guess I deserved that!"

"Seriously, Andy," replied Stringer, "It's not so unusual. This approach is a bitch—even in daylight."

"Yes, I know. I know it so well I should have been more cautious. But, what's done is done; so when we get in, have the base force dive the screws. And, Mike, have them do it immediately if they can. We want this boat ready to go out again as soon as possible.

After a brief wait for a change in the tidal condition—fortunately a rise—the damaged PT pulled itself off the inhospitable coral, resumed its course to and across the bay, then up the sinuous inlet to the advanced base.

As they began passing the non-patrolling boats moored in and under the mangroves, an early-rising officer signalled a questioning "thumbs up?"—to which Andy replied with a disconsolate shake of the head and a responding "thumbs down."

Miss Sing You slipped alongside the main dock, lines were secured, and McCloud jumped ashore, turning back to his exec.

"Mike, besides getting that screw—or screws—replaced, gas her up. As I said, we could well be going out later on."

Stopping at one of the showers, he cracked the tap and, filling his outstretched hands, rinsed hands and face, ran fingers through his hair, then turned to the steep trail leading up the hill to the squadron commander's hut. Deep in concentration, he barely missed stepping on a yard-long asp taking advantage of the warmth of the early sun. Drawing back abruptly, he gained an early-morning salute from the reptile: it reared, mouth agape, uttering a less-than-friendly hiss before slithering off into a white-blossomed frangipani.

The squadron commander's palm-frond bedecked hut was built on a raised wooden platform, an armed sailor looking down on McCloud's approach. McCloud returned his salute, stepped up to the screened door, rapped, waited, then continued rapping until Lieutenant Commander Winters appeared at the bedroom door, heavy-eyed and skivvy-clad.

McCloud smiled to himself. I've never seen the boss like this, he thought. Ordinarily he's the combed, bathed, and starched epitome of an Annapolis graduate. Guess the old boy is human after all!

"McCloud!" mouthed the awakening squadron commander. "Good Lord, you're an early one! Good tidings the cause of it, I hope?"

"Good news? Some, yes, Sir—and some bad, too."

"Both, eh? Well, come in and have a seat. I'll be with you momentarily."

A few minutes later, a transformed commanding officer appeared—a few wet spots appearing through his khaki shirt attesting to the haste of his ablutions. Dropping into his desk chair, he swiveled around to face the boat captain.

"Now, good morning again, McCloud. Tell me—what happened? Is Jollymore all right?"

"Yes, Sir. That part of it went without a hitch. We put him ashore per schedule and apparently he's on his way up to, or already at, his hideaway."

"Fine. But, then, what's the bad news?"

"The worst kind, Commander. We lost a man."

"Lost a man? Tell me about it."

Andy McCloud summarized the details of the night: the loss of, and futile search for, Markowski.

"Anything further, Andy? You indicated there's more."

"Yes, Sir. It's just that we hit a reef coming through those damnable reefs outside of the bay and damaged at least one screw."

"Who had the con?"

"I did. Sir, I goofed."

"You did! You of all people. I'm surprised. But, after all, that can be repaired."

"Yes, Sir—and, hopefully, they're at it now."

"Now, Andy, back to the more serious business about the loss of that man of yours—Markowski you said. Any suggestions?"

"Yes, Sir. It was blacker than the bottom of a coal bin at midnight out there—no moon at all. He could be floating around and we simply missed him. If you can arrange for the Air Force to give us some cover, I'd like to go back out there in daylight as soon as the underwater gear is repaired, that is."

"Oh no, McCloud. Negative to that. That would most certainly alert the Japs to the fact that something unusual has been going on in the area. We simply can't do anything that would put Jollymore in more danger than he's already in. No, that's out. But perhaps we can do part of it. I'll ask the pilots to swing by the area today and keep an eye peeled for Markowski. Then, if anything comes of it, we'll take it from there."

"Aye aye, Sir," came the grudging response.

"Although," continued Winters, "I'll tell you what you can do. Normally, you wouldn't be patrolling tonight. But just in case we hear anything positive from the Air Force, get your boat in shape, try to give the crew a bit of rest, and I'll keep in touch with you."

"Okay, Commander. Wilco to that."

"And one more thing, Andy. I can imagine how you must feel. I'm sorry it happened—the loss of your man, I mean."

"Thank you. Sir."

Μ cCloud went back down the trail, coming upon his boat at the main dock—with the red flag of Baker at the mainmast indicating refueling underway.

I just hope the locals here have been properly indoctrinated, he mused. He couldn't help but recall the loss of two boats at Tufi--their former base down the coast—due to the careless toss of a cigarette by an uninformed native.

Seeing Stringer on the bow, McCloud told him about his conversation with the squadron commander, then inquired about the status of repairs to the underwater gear.

"Taken care of, Andy. They plan to get at it about ten hundred hours this morning—said the tide would be just right at that time. I didn't want to display my ignorance to that base force group, but tell me, Andy, what does the tide have to do with it?"

McCloud grinned. "You needn't have worried, Mike—it's a local peculiarity. Those chickens—being allergic to crocodiles—have rigged an underwater circular cyclone fence in the river over there near the other bank. We'll position her stern—if *Miss Sing You* will pardon the innuendo—over the fencing and when the tide is right, she should squat down on it. Then if all goes well, they can check and replace the damaged prop, or props, with impunity."

"You mean those big, manly base force types are afraid of little old crocodiles?"

"It isn't the 'little old ones' they worry about, Mike, but since Baedeker says this area raises the largest crocs in the world—some measuring well over twenty feet—the answer is 'hell yes!'"

"Oh, brother! That I can understand. But, Andy, you said 'if all goes well.' What did you mean by that?"

"Oh that. It just means if they haven't put the cyclone fencing *around* one!"

— —

Since nothing positive had been heard from the Air Force patrols, no search was scheduled for the evening.

The crew of the 150 was gathered on the forecastle, avidly surrounding a punch bowl containing the juice of locally-picked limes and, with the understanding and clandestine acquiescence of McCloud, a generous lacing of distilled torpedo alcohol—"torpedo juice" in their vernacular. Habitual conversation was sparse, the men long-faced, morose, and contemplative. Normal bantering was wanting until the alcohol took effect and the usual topic— "girls, what we did with them and how much we miss them"— was finally broached. But, even then, the usual braggarts remained unnaturally quiescent.

The two boat officers appeared topside, and with that, one of the seamen put down his cup and approached the bridge. Touching his cap, he said, "Skipper, could I have a word with you?"

"Sure, Krug, but is it anything Mr. Stringer shouldn't be privy to?"

"Pri...privy...I don't understand. Sir. That's what we called the head when I went to scout camp."

McCloud grinned. "In this case, Krug, you will be *relieved* to know I mean is it anything Mr. Stringer shouldn't be in on?"

"Oh no, Sir," said Krug, "that makes it twice as good."

McCloud's smile broadened. "Krug, are you planning on making the Navy a career?"

The seaman shook his head. "No, Sir. I'm just in for the war. But why do you ask, Sir?"

"Because with a ready reply like you just gave us, you may be right in shrugging off the Navy for something else—like politics for instance. Ever thought of that?"

"N—no Sir, I haven't."

"All right. We'll leave that right there. Now, we'll be glad to hear what you have to say—on one condition, that is."

"Yes, Sir?"

"That you go back to that punch bowl with these two cups and bring us our ration."

Krug brightened. "Aye aye, Sir. I'll be right back."

As Krug approached the punch bowl, one of the crew nudged another and, with a grin, surreptitiously pointed at the two cups. The nudgee returned the smile and nodded.

Krug returned to the bridge with the two cups. The officers tasted the punch appreciatively.

"Mmmmm, good," said Stringer. "Must have been a great vintage year."

McCloud set his cup down next to the compass. "Now, now go ahead, Krug. What's on your mind?"

"Well, Sir, it's about Markowski. I don't know how well you know—or knew him—but he's a bit of a weirdo."

"A *weirdo*? In what way?"

"Well, Sir, he hates Japs."

"What's so weird about that? Isn't that pretty well true of all of us? After all, they've earned it."

Krug nodded. "Sure, Skipper, but not like this guy. He's wild-eyed on the subject. That's all he talks about. That and the fact that he just wants to kill Japs because of what they did to his father. You know they killed him—his father—at the start of the war in the Philippines, don't you?"

"Yes again, Krug. That's a tough one. But, then, a lot of us suffered losses of one kind or another at that time. And, because of it, isn't that why we're here? It's our assignment—and what we want to do."

"Sure, Skipper. You're sure right about that. But, this guy Markowski—he *lives* for it. He wants to get them with his bare hands—to strangle them one by one."

"Well, come to think about it, he seems capable of it. He's pretty brawny."

"Yes, Sir, you're certainly right about that. Sir. You know those big biceps of his—especially the one with the naked dame tattooed on it? Do you know when he clenches and unclenches his fist, she does a first-class hula?"

"Is that right, Krug?"

"Yes, Sir, it sure is. And do you know. Sir, he isn't even happy when we do get some of them—the Japs, that is. He keeps bitching that, down there in the engine room, he can't even *see* what's going on topside."

"Do you think that's what happened? That he came topside to see what was going on and fell overboard?"

"Gee, I don't know, Sir. But I suppose it could have happened that way."

Mike Stringer broke in. "It sounds to me like Markowski is in the wrong outfit. He should have joined the Marine Corps, like his father."

"Oh, he tried that first, Sir," replied Krug, "but for some reason he couldn't make it—said it was something about not getting along well with the doc."

"Do you know what he meant? In what way couldn't he get along with the doctor?"

The question seemed to bother Krug. "I think...I believe...as I remember it. Sir, the doc asked Markowski how often he masturbated—and Markowski told him he didn't think it was any of his goldarned business. Besides that, the doc found out that Markowski wasn't old enough to enlist without his mother's permission, and she wouldn't give it to him. Said something about having already lost a husband in the war, and she didn't want to lose a son too."

"What happened then, Krug? How did he get in the Navy?"

"I asked him about that. He said he still wanted to get back at the Japs because of his dad, so he went back to the courthouse and down the hall to the Navy recruiting office and lied again—this time to guys he described as 'a helluva nice chief petty officer and his sawbones—a different type this time.' Somehow they found out he had tried to get in the Marines, and when they asked him about it, he lied again. Told them that was right, but the reason he didn't go through with it was because he had changed his mind and decided he'd rather be in the Navy—especially if he could get into PT boats."

"And they believed him?"

"Yes, Sir, they did—hook, line, and sinker. And, as a matter of fact, he said the chief told him he had made a good choice—said the Marines got that stripe down their pant leg 'cause they're pissin' posts for the Navy.'"

"Are you quoting Markowski on that," asked McCloud, "or is that what you believe, Krug?"

"N—no, Sir," stammered Krug. "I was just—just reporting what Markowski told me."

"I'm glad to hear that, Krug. I know it's popular for the Navy to make fun of the Marines—and vice versa—but if it comes from anyone else, I think you'd soon find the Navy is awfully proud of their 'soldiers of the sea.'"

"Yes, Sir—I know what you mean, Sir."

"All right, Krug. Thanks for the information. Before you go, isn't it true you're from Wisconsin?"

"Yes, Sir, Skipper—from Packerland: Green Bay."

"That's beer country, isn't it, Krug?"

"Yes, Sir, that and cheese."

"Then you should know that only having one of these things," said McCloud pointing at his cup, "is apt to throw one badly out of balance. Do you think you could refuel them for us?"

"Yes, Sir," grinned Krug. "I'd be glad to."

When Krug left, McCloud turned to Stringer. "A fine young man that. Hey, look who's here."

Childers, the squadron commander's yeoman stood on the bank looking up at the bridge. "Lieutenant McCloud, Sir—the Commander wants to see you."

"Now?"

"Yes, Sir. 'Now,' he said."

"Tell him I'll be up as soon as possible."

Childers left. McCloud reached for the cup Krug was handing him and turned to his executive officer. "It's a difficult decision, but, as they say, 'first things first' — down the hatch, Mike."

— —

Night was closing in rapidly, and, despite the appearance of a crescent moon, McCloud left the boat and negotiated the uphill trail with flashlight in hand.

"Commander, Sir, you wanted to see me?"

Lieutenant Commander Winters swiveled around from his desk. "Ah, that was commendably prompt, McCloud. Come in and have a seat. We have news—news from friend Jollymore."

"He didn't waste any time getting back on the air, did he, Commander?"

"No, he certainly didn't. Competent fellow, that. Says he's all set in that department, but he wants to see us, for two reasons. First, he wants us to pick up Donegal tomorrow night—apparently the fellow *is* 'troppo,' if you know what that means. And, secondly, he says he has news of Markowski."

"Markowski! What's the news?"

"I don't know at this point. Evidently it's rather lengthy and, as you know, these coastwatchers don't want to stay on the air any longer than they have to. You understand why, don't you?"

"Yes, Sir, I most certainly do."

"We'll learn more when we see him tomorrow night— same time, same place."

"You said 'we,' Commander. You're going with us?"

"Yes, that's right. Just tell me your estimated time of departure. Probably the same as last night. Right?"

"Yes, Sir, that's right. That will be 1930—a bit early to allow for contingencies. And, we'll break out your burgee."

"You've got to be kidding, Andy. No publicity in the war zone, thank you."

5

Weather conditions the following evening proved a near duplicate of the former patrol: unusually rough seas directly on the bow but slightly better visibility, thanks to the aid of the new moon. McCloud, Stringer, and squadron leader Winters were aboard *Miss Sing You*, with Paul Corbett and his 143 boat—*Miss Guidance*—in column astern.

A covert glance by McCloud showed the squadron commander next to him on the bridge, grinning slightly into the wind.

"Excuse me, Commander, but you seem to be enjoying this god-awful chop. I take it you like a rough sea?"

"Not particularly, Andy, but after all the time my current assignment keeps me land-bound in that shack up the hill, any opportunity to ride the boats is pure pleasure. By the way, how are we doing as far as time is concerned?"

"As I mentioned yesterday, our plan was to leave a bit early to allow for contingencies, and we did. We're right on that schedule. Sir."

The squadron commander nodded. "I'm more than a bit suspicious that some of you feather merchants have somehow discovered what we learned our first year at the Academy: If you have a designated time of arrival, be sure and get to your destination early, hang just over the horizon then dash in at the last minute and collect accolades for your superior navigation. Am I right, Andy?"

"Oh come now, Commander, we would never fabricate a plan such as that—or are you recommending it?"

"Why...ahem...of course not. I was just engaging in a bit of levity. Now, to get back to tonight's mission. Have you two given any more thought to the matter of Jollymore's reference to Markowski?"

"I sure have, Commander," replied McCloud, "and it bothers the hell out of me."

"Bothers you? What do you mean?"

"Simply this, Sir: I can't understand how Jollymore could have any information about him—Markowski, that is. Hell, Commander, Jollymore didn't even know he was missing—unless you told him on the air. After all, we only discovered his absence *after* we put Jollymore ashore!"

"Well first, he didn't learn it from me. And second, you're dead right, Andy. That is peculiar!"

As they neared their now-familiar landfall in the lee corner of the Huon Gulf, sea conditions moderated as expected. The cliffs and the sand beach at their foot were delineated more clearly than on their previous visit. With the same blanket of stars above, plus the crescent moon astern, it should, thought Andy McCloud—and with it, even more need for caution.

After lying to for a spell (almost like the Commander's Annapolis story, thought McCloud) engines were muffled and Corbett and his 143 boat were left behind as the 150 began its quiet idle toward the now-familiar beachhead—all stations at General Quarters, manned and ready.

"McCloud," murmured the squadron commander, "Are you planning on taking it right in to the beach? You did it the other night, didn't you?"

"Yes, Sir, and it worked well—found a sand beach with ample water. And, having an even higher tide tonight, it shouldn't be any problem at all."

As they neared the alien shore, McCloud looked at his watch and grinned. "Commander, this 'feather merchant' is right on time, so, here we go."

As before, *Miss Sing You* nosed gently onto the sand, the Jacob's ladder was thrown over the bow, and simultaneously three figures emerged from the mangroves fringing the beach: Jim Jollymore, a stocky companion whom the Americans assumed was his predecessor and their proposed passenger for the return to Morobe, and a colorfully-clad native—if 'colorfully clad' is apropos in describing a lone burnt-ocher armlet and matching supporter known as a "laplap" to the locals. Jollymore waved and he and his companion came down the beach to the PT where two crewmen waited at the bottom of the Jacob's ladder to assist them.

When the duo reached the forecastle, Lieutenant Commander Winters put out his hand. "Welcome aboard, Jim. It's good to see you again."

"Jolly glad to be here, Commander—for the most part, that is. And this is Jerry Donegal, who will be going back with you."

"And pleased to meet you face-to-face at last, Jerry," said Winters, shaking hands with and studying the coastwatcher's careworn countenance. Jim Jollymore's description seemed appropriate, he thought. The man does look "troppo"—and after all he's gone through this past year, who can be critical of him?

"I know you've been out here a long time. Jerry, and believe me, all you've done for us in the interim is deeply appreciated."

"Get away with you. Commander. Working with you fellows has been a ripper."

"'Ripper,' eh," smiled Winters. "That goes both ways." He motioned toward his companions. "This is our boat captain, Andy McCloud... and this, the executive officer, Mike Stringer." Both greeted him with firm handshakes.

"Now, I suggest we go to the bridge for a bit more privacy." He pointed up and down the beach, then at the cliffs above. "Frankly, I feel like we're sharing this with our Nipponese neighbors."

"I don't know about that 'neighbors' bit," said Donegal, "but knowing those yobbos like I do, it wouldn't surprise me if we were."

With the three officers and the two coastwatchers together on the bridge, Gordon Winters said, "All right, Jim, tell us the rest of the story. How are things with you?"

"Everything's fair dinkum up above. Commander. Just as I thought—the squaller needed a touch or two, but just as you know, it's good-oh now. Jerry here has the bushies in bonzer shape—but he's been up there in the never-never a long time. He's earned a bit of spinebashing."

The squadron commander shook his head and smiled. "'Spinebashing'—what in the world is that?"

Jollymore returned the smile. "Commander, you've just proved I was right in warning Jerry about your lack of linguistic enlightenment. Now, as to that

40

'spinebashing,' that's up front English. Just means the man needs a rest—and, as I said, he's earned it."

"Okay," said Winters. "You win again, Jim. Now tell us the rest of the story. You said you had problems."

"S'treuth is, I don't have any personal problems—except those stirred up by that drop kick of yours named Markowski."

"Markowski!" broke in Andy McCloud. "He's here?"

Jim Jollymore glanced at Donegal, then grimaced. "Oh he's here all right—bigger than life and twice the trouble. That boofhead of yours isn't the full quid—he's giving us the shits!"

"Good Lord," said McCloud. "How did he get here? We figured we'd lost him overboard and have been searching for him ever since!"

"Lost him overboard is close, Andy, but not quite the way you mean it. Oh, he slid over the side all right—the other side of this boat that is while you were busy putting me ashore. That he did, mate —carbine, machete, tuckerbag, and all!"

"Carbine! Machete! For what? What in the world is he doing?"

"What is he doing? Believe it or not, that imbo thinks he's a bloody one-man army. And, not only thinks it, but he's trying to carry it out. He's off trying to kill Japs—the lot of them! And, worst of all, he keeps coming back to see us! As you know, we need a drop-in like him like...like...What is it you Yanks say? Like we need a hole in the head!"

Winters broke in, "But why, Jim? Why does he keep bothering you?"

"Well, it seems the imbo has already run out of food, and wants rest and companionship as well. And since we

41

seem to be the only place he knows to find all three, we're stuck with him."

The anguished coastwatcher turned to Winters with outspread hands. "Commander, it's like I told you back at your base. We're Ferdinands. Our sole mission is to sit quietly and not disturb anyone—never create a ruckus—just watch the Nips and report what they're up to. But, this yobbo of yours is running around like a chook with its head cut off, attracting a helluva lot of Nip attention, then crawling back to us for his R and R, with the Nips trying to follow him. Commander, you've *got* to get him the hell out of here before he buggers up the whole deal—for both of us!"

"Of course we do, Jim—and will, one way or another." Winters turned to McCloud. "How do you suggest we do it, Andy? Got any ideas?"

"You bet I do, Commander. Since Markowski's *my* responsibility, I'll go back up with Jim and retrieve him."

"No, Andy—no, that won't do at all. You've got a boat to run."

Mike Stringer stepped forward, hand raised. "But I don't, Commander. I'm kind of like Markowski thought he was. I'm excess baggage. Let me do the job."

Winters looked Stringer up and down appraisingly— and appreciatively—then glanced at McCloud, who nodded reluctantly. He tuned back to Jollymore. "Would that be all right with you, Jim—that is, if Ensign Stringer here plus a volunteer from the crew—goes back up with you?"

"Sure would, Commander—t'would be a beauty. Anything that gets that dropkick out of here before he buggers up the whole war!"

The squadron commander turned to the executive officer. "All right, Stringer. We appreciate what you're offering to do. Now, see if you can find a capable volunteer to go up with you."

"Aye aye, Sir. I believe I know just the man."

Stringer reported back in a surprisingly short time, a barrel-chested crewman at his side. "Commander, this is Bosun's Mate Zachary."

Gordon Winters eyed the boatswain's mate critically — and apparently the man passed muster. "Glad to meet you, Zachary. I gather you're volunteering to go ashore with Mr. Stringer?"

The stocky, muscular, and mustachioed Zachary glanced at the executive officer, then grinned. "Yes Sir, Commander, you could put it that way."

"Fine," nodded Winters, turning back to the coastwatcher. "Now, Jim, tell them what they will need in the way of equipment."

"Well, mates, it's hard to tell just when we'll see that shipmate of yours. Thus far, it's been every day or two, but who can tell? Knowing that imbo, anything could change.

"But first, it's not a simple jaunt up to our place, so you'll need comfortable clothing. I'd say a jacket, walking shoes or boots, and bare essential toilet gear. Oh — and one more thing. I like to carry a machete, as you can see. If you have any aboard, you each might want to bring one."

"Why the machete, Jim?" queried Stringer.

"Well, first, they're kind of handy for a lot of things here in the bush — brushing out an overgrown trail, for instance. And, as you'll see, I'm using the word 'trail' loosely. So loosely, the bloody asps seem to think it belongs to them, and I find it necessary to send them to snake heaven with the machete. Then, too, here in Nipland, they're not like a gun—they're nice and quiet." He turned to Donegal. "Did I miss anything. Jerry?"

"Troppo" Donegal came alive. "Oh my, yes—you left out one of the most important ones—the nosh department. Maybe they could pack a supply of din-din—like that great tucker they get in cans."

Mike Stringer interrupted him. "Great tucker in cans? Meat, you mean? By any chance, could you be referring to Spam?"

"That's rightoh, mate—it's a great spread."

Skinner put a hand on his stomach and groaned. "It might be for a newcomer like you, Jerry, but we've had it a thousand times and disguised a hundred ways. But, no sir, you can't fool these taste buds any longer. They'd know that old friend in any crowd. Why, I'd even prefer to live on those coconuts of yours for a few days!"

"In that case," laughed Jollymore, "you've got yourself a deal. It's nuts to you, and I'll sacrifice myself and take the Spam."

Squadron Commander Winters put up his hand. "Quickly now, let's move this thing along. Have Cookee throw some chow together—yes, including the Spam. And, Mike, two other things. If you're as allergic as I am to malaria, I'd take some mosquito netting if you have any aboard."

"That we have, Sir," said McCloud.

"It's a bonzer thought," added Jollymore, "enough for all of us, I hope."

"No problem."

"One more thought," said Winters. "You'll need side-arms and a set of handcuffs. Markowski's to be put under arrest immediately. If he asks what for, tell him 'desertion in time of war.' But, the main thing is to be sure and bring him down here."

"Aye aye, Sir."

"And Jim, when they have him, let us know. We'll meet them here the night we hear from you—same place and time."

"Aye, Commander," said the broadly grinning Jollymore, "t'will be a ripper."

6

The introspectively engrossed trio: Jim Jollymore, Mike Stringer, and Boatswain's Mate Zachary watched the PT pull off the beach, come about, then head out to sea.

Stringer broke the silence. "Well, that's it, fellows. Let's get going. Lead on, Jim."

"Lead on?" queried Jollymore. "No way. You wouldn't want to try that trail tonight, mates. It's bad enough on a full moonlit night. But tonight with that sliver, no. As you'll see come morning, it's rough enough in full daylight. We'll just sack out until first light."

"Sack out? Where? Certainly not here on the beach!"

"Aye mate, here on the beach. You wouldn't enjoy stretching out in that bush. It's full of everything that creeps, crawls, slithers, and bites. Unless you're well equipped for it—and we're not—we're better off to go to the top of the beach, near the bush, but not in it. Just scoop out a nice soft bit of that hard sand for your arse, and try to relax."

"But how about your native friend? Where did he go?"

"Oh, Athnasius? He's different. That trail is downtown Sidney for him. He was just keeping me company. He's gone back up to the cockie for the night. Even if he runs into some Nips, it won't cause any stir at all. And, you'll see him again—up there."

"On that score: how about those Japanese? Aren't they liable to take a midnight stroll along this beach?"

"Aye, could be, mate, and to cover that possibility, I would suggest we set a watch, and divide the night—starting with me. If we see any Nips 'strolling the beach' as you put it, we'll just move back into the bush a tad until they pass. But, keep your guns and machetes handy." Jollymore grinned, "And don't snore too loud."

———

"Fellows," said Mike Stringer in an insistent whisper. "Wake up! It's first light. I think we can get going now."

Jollymore raised his head and peered about. "Aye, mates, that we can." He went to the line of the bush, turned to the brightening eastern sky, and proceeded to relieve himself—promptly joined in synchronous performance by the other two.

"Nothing like a hit and miss," yawned the coastwatcher.

"Hit and miss?" queried Mike Stringer. "Would I be correct in surmising 'rhymes with piss'?"

"Why strike me pink as that dawn! Right on, Mike! Reminds me of something my old man used to say to me on rare occasions: 'Son, you're smarter than you look!' But let's try it again. What if I'd said 'hey diddle diddle?'"

"Could I give it a try, Sir?" asked Zachary.

"Be my guest."

"'Hey diddle diddle' rhymes with 'piddle'?"

Jollymore guffawed. "By Gripes—you too, mate! Why you're smart enough to be an officer!"

Zachary returned the grin. "Officer, no; mate, yes— bosun's mate, that is."

A smiling Mike Stringer raised his idle hand. "Enough of that, you two! Tell us, Jim, when we finish this salute to the dawn, what are your marching orders?"

"That we get off this beach—right now. Let's pack up our gear and take off. I'll take the lead. It's about two miles up to my camp, and fairly rough going in spots— hardly a stroll along King's Cross, you know."

"But," said Zachary, "how about some chow?"

"Sure, mate, we'll need that, but the good guts is there's a billabong half way up where we can catch a breather and have a cool drink while we have a touch of the munchies."

Mike Stringer scratched his head. "You've got me there, Jim. I've heard of it, but tell me: What's a 'billabong'?"

The Australian smirked. "Billabong? Why, that's a spa, mate—you know, a watering hole. You Seppos are all alike—you do have trouble with ordinary English."

"I'm afraid you're right, Jim," smiled Stringer. "But, with you as our guru, we'll gain on it."

Zachary picked up and adjusted the knapsack, then squinted upward. "Not much of a trail you said?"

"No, Zach," said their leader. "But that's all to the good. We wouldn't want to take a highway in this Nip country, would we?" He reached down. "Now, if you'll each latch onto one of these tuckerbags, we can head for the scrub. And, speaking of the Nips, from now on, let's keep our chatter to the minimum. I doubt if we'll run across any of them, but with those dropkicks, you never know."

Jollymore pushed some branches aside and started up the 'trail,' the two Yanks following. They soon found their guide had put it mildly; it was anything but a 'stroll.' The so-called trail was barely discernible and strewn with rocks—slippery devils predisposed to shift, rattle, and roll. The path—if it deserved the appellation at all, meandered around trees and brush, with the grade averaging steep and steeper.

While they were pausing for a breather, Zachary said, "If I'd known what this was going to be like, I'd have worn a pair of shorts instead of these GI's."

"Oh no, mate. This kunai grass is sharp as a razor. You wouldn't have been as happy as you are. If you had, your legs would be a bloody mess by now."

"But, Jim, what about your native friend? That jock strap he's wearing can't even be called 'shorts.'"

"Athnasius? He was born and raised on kunai. His legs are as tough as his feet!"

An errant asp slithered across their way, paused, eyed Jollymore, then raised its head and hissed. With a practiced swing of his machete, the coastwatcher severed its head and returned the hiss. "Take that, Joe Blake!"

"Nice backhand, Jim," breathed Stringer in a sibilant whisper, "and it has to be 'Joe Blake' rhymes with snake?"

Jollymore grinned and returned the whisper. "Righto, Yank—and keep up the good work—you'll be taken for an Aussie yet!"

"Thanks, Jim. I accept that as a compliment. But, tell us, what should we do if the next one's a python?"

"Don't try to lop off its head," grinned Jollymore.

"Pythons have the right of way. Just step back and bow him across."

After what seemed an endless and breathless pre-breakfast struggle to the two Americans—marked only by further spasmodic assassinations of luckless asps, or the passage of yard-long lizards with questioning green eyes—a verdant plateau was reached, a small stream gurgling full-born from the upper rock, then trickling off toward the ocean far below.

"This is it, mates," said their guide in a hoarse whisper. "Now, let me introduce you to a genuine New Guinea billabong. Be my guest—wet your whistles. That water springing out of nature's bubbler is perfectly fit to drink."

"Ha!" laughed Stringer, "'bubbler'—that's a howler!"

"Pardon me, Sir," said Zachary, "There's nothing strange about that. In Green Bay, we've got them on every corner."

"'Drinking fountains' you mean Zachary?"

"No. 'Bubblers,' Sir."

"All right, we'll take your word for it—after all, you're from Northern Wisconsin and that's kind of like being from inner New Guinea, isn't it?"

"Mates!" murmured Jollymore urgently, "Knock it off! Keep your lingo down to a whisper. Remember, we're in Jap country!"

Stringer raised his hands apologetically, Zachary nodded in agreement, and their guide smiled and pointed at the water. The Americans indulged themselves, finding their down-under friend right about the water. "Delushious" Zachary's whisper phrased it.

"By the way," breathed Stringer, "as I remember it, the song goes: 'Once a jolly swagman camped by a billabong.' Tell me, what's a 'swagman'?"

"Oh that," smiled Jollymore, "I thought everyone knew that—even a highly educated Seppo. A swagman is a tramp, a hobo. But now, mates, as soon as you've finished your munchies, we *should* get a move on—unless you *insist* on joining me for a bit more of a breather!"

Turning to Ensign Stringer, Zachary sighed, "Oh man, all this might be a piece of cake for an officer, but it's not for a swabbie like me. I was afraid he wouldn't suggest it. Frankly, Sir, I'm pooped. I thought I was in pretty good shape, but I guess playing around on that eighty-foot boat is lousy training for shinnying up a mountain."

Mike Stringer, relieved that the boatswain's mate had expressed himself first, lowered his tuckerbag and slumped to the grass.

"Right on, Zach. Your analysis is impeccable."

"I'm not sure about that 'impeccable' bit," said Jollymore, "but you Yanks are not alone. It's always this way for me. Whenever I get to this billibong, I feel weaker than a sunburned snowflake."

Stringer chuckled. "The man's positively eloquent, isn't he, Zach?"

"That he is, Sir. I'm going to remember that 'sunburned snowflake' bit. Right now, it fits me to a tee."

Momentarily, the sun burst over the horizon, engulfing the area in light. With a rustle of leaves, a large auburn and gold bird with magnificent, improbably long, yellow tail feathers dropped from a nearby tree; then gaining airspeed, it soared overhead, making the Elysian scene complete.

"Oh brother!" said Zachary in an awed whisper. "Fantastic!"

51

"Right on, Zach," said Jollymore. "Let's take it as a good omen—a salute to a promising day from one of the world's most beautiful critters."

"Agreed. But what is it?"

"Why that, mate, that's a bird of paradise in full plumage."

"Well, it may be the most beautiful to look at, but back at Morobe we've got one with more talent. It's equipped with awesome armpits, and every time it beats its wings, it sounds like a mighty fart."

"Ah, I know the one you mean," laughed Stringer. "We call it 'the bird with the pneumatic armpits.'"

"That's the difference between us. It might be 'pneumatic armpits' to you officers, but to us swab jockeys, it's just plain old booming farts—Sir."

When they finished their brunch —'nosh' in Jim Jollymore's patois—plus a bit of rest, their leader rose and bent over the 'bubbler' for a final drink. "One more before we go—those others hardly touched my sides." After a long swallow, he straightened up. "Ready mates? We really ought to get up there and take a gander at what the Nips are up to this morning."

"All set, Jim," said Mike Stringer. "But, tell us what it's like—the rest of the climb, that is. Tough as the first part?"

"Oh no," smiled Jollymore. "You'll be pleased to know the worst is behind us—temporarily, that is. It's sort of a walk in the park until we get to my old place— the cokey cockie. Then, I must admit, it's a bit of a struggle up to the lookout."

As predicted, the rest of the climb was somewhat easier, but difficult enough to give Zachary another chance to grouse.

"This may be 'just a walk in the park' to you, Jim, but *Central* Park, it ain't!"

Finally, the terrain leveled out into what obviously was an overgrown coconut plantation.

"Here it is, mates—my old cockie. I hate to have you seeing it looking like a dog's breakfast. Donegal said that some of my old boys have been doing their best to keep it up, but apparently the Nips have other ideas of what's important."

Mike Stringer looked around, then asked, "Is this where your camp is, Jim?"

"Oh, go on with you! Lord, no! Come on—we'll amble through this bit of the cocky, then back into the bush and up to the lookout and my camp. But, right now you're about to discover I'm an up-front sort of chap. You won't enjoy the stroll, but just keep telling yourselves it's not likely the Nips will stumble onto it. That'll level it out."

The 'stroll' proved the precision of Jollymore's word by being the most torturous yet encountered, with the final segment requiring a single-file procession between, over, and around boulders interspersed in a series of crags—an obstacle course of the most arduous order.

Arriving at a sudden outcropping to the northwest, Jollymore said, "Come on over to the outer edge of this."

Stringer and Zachary did as directed.

"There," said Jollymore with a sweep of his arm. "There are the playmates who gave you Pearl Harbor." Spread out below was the deltoid panorama of Lae—harbor, town, airfield, and all.

"Wonderful!" breathed Mike Stringer. "What a marvelous view! I can see why Jerry was so effective. Every plane, every ship, every sub—even every barge. Nothing could get into or out of that place undetected!"

"You're right, Mike—as long as we have good weather, that is. And like this day, we usually do in this season."

"But, when you have something to report you have to go to your camp, don't you? Where is it? And where's the radio?"

"Oh, we wouldn't have any of that here!"

"You wouldn't? Why not?"

"No, Mike—if the Nips suspected they were being watched, this would have to be one of he places they'd investigate to find whoever was doing the watching. S'treuth, this is one of the best viewpoints we have, but I think you can understand we don't want to leave a trace of our presence here—or at any of our other lookouts. As you will see, our camp and radio are a bit of a ways away, well hidden in a spot where the terrain seems to block our transmissions from any big ears down there at Lae—we hope. Come on, mates. Let's go down there now."

As they backed off the viewpoint, Jollymore picked up a nearby branch and swept away any trace of their presence.

With gear in hand and on backs, they followed Jollymore part way down the rocky spire, then threaded their way several hundred even more unobtrusive yards along the back of a promontory to, and along another single-file gradation, finally arriving at a well-concealed shallow cavern facing eastward, away from Lae. Upon further inspection, it proved surprisingly well-equipped for a passable existence.

"Welcome to Jerry's—and now my abode. Pull up a rock and make yourselves comfortable."

"But," objected Mike Stringer, "what about our mission? What about Markowski? How do we go about finding him?"

"Oh, there's nothing we can do about *finding* that imbo. Lord knows where he's hunting Nips today. All we can do is wait for him to come to *us*, and judging by what I've seen, that he'll do, by jingo, unless they—the Nips—get him first. But, the good oil is, that doesn't bother me as much as the possibility of him leading them back up here and buggering up our whole operation."

"But, Jim, how did he ever find this place of yours?"

"After you left me off—and, unknown to you, the imbo at the same time—he just trailed us. And by cripes, you have to give him some credit. Even with Athnasius with me, I never suspected we were being followed."

Mike Stringer nodded. "I see. And how often do you see him?"

"That's hard to say, Mike. Thus far it's been every day. But whether he'll turn up in ten minutes or ten hours—or even turn up at all today—I can't say. And, of course, if the Nips get him, our problem is solved."

"There's another thing I don't understand, Jim. When Markowski does show up, you don't welcome him with open arms, do you?"

"Hell's bell—no!"

"Well, then, if that's the case, why does he come here at all?"

"That, Mike, is a bonzer question. Even though he must know he browns us off, I guess he's got no alternative. I guess he just plain gets hungry: for nosh, rest and maybe companionship—although, believe me, mates, from me, he's having a hard time getting any of it, especially that 'companionship' bit."

"If that's the case, I still don't understand why he continues to show up."

"By cripes, I don't either! But, that boofhead of yours so far just doesn't take 'no' for an answer. And, fellows, the full bob is that sooner or later—*sooner*, I'm afraid,— he's going to bugger up our whole show. Why, it was just two days ago when Athnasius, the only remaining one doing his best to take care of my old cockie, came up here to tell me a group of Nips, mad as cut snakes—came up to the cockie looking for that imbo of yours. They didn't find him, so they shot a buddy of Athnasius'. By cripes, mates, that's getting too close for comfort."

A sudden roar of engines brought the trio to the entrance of the hideaway to witness dozens of planes. The Japanese "Val" dive bombers and their escorting Zero fighters passed close overhead, then disappeared behind the promontory, obviously arcing down toward the port of Lae.

"Strike me pink!" gasped Jim Jollymore. "Business is picking up! That's the biggest group I've seen or heard of since I've been up here. I'm going up to have a seesaw."

"Mind if we join you, Jim?" asked Stringer.

"Well—okay, mates. With all this fuss, I guess it'll be okay. Come along."

With Jollymore leading the way, the trio scrambled back up to the observation point—the same precariously posed one they had visited earlier in the day.

"Look! Look at that!" glowed Jollymore, pointing down at the airstrip. "How many are there? I count— let's see—thirty-two and lined up like birds in a shooting gallery—exactly what they'll be if we can get the word to your flyboys at that Dobodura strip near Buna. Come on, mates, let's get back down to the base and crank up the squawker. The fun's about to start!"

Back down in the cavern, Jim Jollymore threw switches, and while waiting for the teleradio to warm up, pushed a large antenna out of the mouth of the hideaway. Picking up a microphone, he winked at his companions, then spoke.

"Ferdinand Leader, this is Jolly-ex-Don. Thirty-two red balls just landed—lined up for the taking. Repeat: This is Jolly-ex-Don. Good hunting, mates."

"Fascinating, Jim," said Mike Stringer. "But, tell us, what is this Jolly-ex-Don nametag?"

"Oh that. We use the first syllables of our surnames as call letters. That way, they—our fellows—know who we are. And if they know *who* we are, they know *where* we are. And since I'm new here, I'm using the 'ex-Don' addition until they get used to the fact that I've replaced Donegal."

"But, Jim, you spoke of alerting our fellows at the Dobodura strip, yet you called 'Ferdinand Leader.' How do the flyboys get the word?"

"Oh, they should already have it. Your chaps down there are monitoring our Ferdinand frequency, and others are, too. I would be surprised if your base isn't doing the same. At any rate, Eric in Townsville will be following up on it. He doesn't miss any tricks—and with the size of this one, you can be sure he won't!"

"And what do you do now?"

"Nothing. Just sit and wait. Except I'll be going back up in a bit and see the show that's bound to come."

"What about us? Can we see the next act?"

"Mike, I would suggest you stay here this time—just in case the Nips picked up that little message of mine and see me and come calling. Understand, mates, with three of us there'd be more to see. Now, if you'll help me pull in that antenna, I'll leave you. And no matter what you hear or see, just sit tight and I'll be in touch with you."

About an hour later, the two Yankees heard sounds of approaching aircraft. This time, the Emperor's red "meatballs" were supplanted by the white stars of American B25's and their escorting P38's. The bombers powered over in a steep dive toward their sitting prey, followed by a crescendo of distant anti-aircraft fire and exploding bombs.

Shortly thereafter, an elated Jim Jollymore appeared.

"What happened?" asked Mike Stringer.

"Plenty! Just be good chaps and lend a hand," replied the grinning coastwatcher. "Swing out that antenna and you'll be in on the answer to your question."

With the antenna deployed and the teleradio warmed up, Jollymore picked up the microphone.

"This is Jolly-ex-Don. Good on you, Yanks. There were thirty-two—now only five." Turning off the set, he turned and grinned anew. "There, mates, you have your answer. Now, if you veterans will be good enough to haul the antenna back in, we'll wait for what you could call 'the next act of the show.'"

"How about our fellows? Did we lose any?"

"Not as far as I could see—although one of the bombers was trailing smoke as they left."

After another interlude, the sound of airplane engines again reverberated off the cavern walls and a dozen American dive bombers screamed overhead, then down in a determined thrust toward the strip at Lae. Jollymore gave his guests a wave and left to "take another optic."

A short interlude later, he returned, gave a thumbs up, and switched on the radio as his new companions pushed the antenna out to its transmission position, returning to hear the news. It was prompt and succinct.

"This is Jolly-ex-Don. Good on you. Yanks. Your job is finished."

Stringer and Zachary turned to retrieve the antenna, but paused. A figure was silhouetted in the cavern entrance.

Markowski.

7

Momentarily, all was silent. Jollymore joined the two Yanks in studying their former shipmate. Markowski stood, mouth agape, rubbed his eyes, and peered in again.

Finally, Mike Stringer broke the silence. "Welcome, Markowski. We've been expecting you."

Markowski continued to squint, probing the depths of the cavern. "But, but I didn't expect—I don't know what to say!"

"You don't have to say anything—but we do. You're under arrest."

"Under arrest! What for?"

"What for! I don't know the complete story at this point, but Commander Winters suggested we use 'desertion' for a starter. And, Markowski, that's one of the most serious of all Navy crimes—especially 'desertion in time of war'."

"Desertion!" murmured Markowski wonderingly, turning as if about to leave.

Mike Stringer drew his revolver. "Hold it right there, Markowski. Don't compound the crime—you're in deep enough hot water as it is. And, if you're having trouble seeing in here, this is a 45 in my hand, and the thing in Zachary's hand is another of the same. Now, if you don't want to add 'resisting arrest' to that desertion charge, be a smart fellow. Put down that carbine and machete, and come in here."

Markowski did as he was told, putting down the weapons, then walked hesitatingly into the cavern. Stringer and Zachary noted the changes in their recalcitrant shipmate's presence: khakis the worse for wear, GI shoes badly scuffed, an eighteen-year-old's peachfuzz in need of a razor, and a sullen frown predominating.

Stringer continued, "Sit over there; that's right—on that rock. Now, Markowski, you have a choice: Stay seated right where you are unless we tell you otherwise, or we can handcuff you to a post. Which would you prefer?"

"Oh, I'll...I'll take the first. I wouldn't like to be handcuffed, Sir."

"Good choice," said Stringer. "Keep it up. Now, tell us: Where did you get that carbine?"

Markowski shook his head. "I'd rather not say, Sir."

"In that case, let me answer for you," said Zachary. "We weren't issued any carbines. The only one aboard was one the skipper had in his locker—the one given to him as a 'thank you' present by that Marine captain who went out with us a few weeks ago. You stole it, didn't you, Leon?"

"Same answer, old pal. If I'm under arrest, I'd rather not answer that—or anything else."

"Okay," nodded Mike Stringer. "Suit yourself, Markowski. You can be cooperative—or play like a sea lawyer. Frankly, though, I can hardly blame you for not wanting to admit to stealing government property. You've got your hands full as it is."

Stringer turned to Jollymore. "Jim, can you tell Commander Winters our mission is accomplished and we'd like to be picked up—tonight, if possible?"

"Sure, mate," replied the coastwatcher. "You understand we're on a fixed frequency aimed at our Townsville headquarters. But if your base is monitoring it—and they certainly should be at this time—it shouldn't be a problem. Now, if you'll do me the favor of goosing that antenna once again, I'll warm this thing up and get right on with it."

Stringer and Zachary rose to do his bidding. Markowski started to get up as well, but Stringer's cautioning hand settled him back on his rock.

The antenna was pushed out to its operable position, the coastwatcher flipped a switch on the teleradio, waited a few moments, then spoke.

"Ferdinand, this is Jolly-ex-Don. The Stringer-Markowski mission has been accomplished and they're ready to go—same place, same time, tonight, unless we hear otherwise."

Flipping the switch off, Jollymore turned to his guests and their prisoner. "All right, mates. You should get going in a couple of hours—which leaves plenty of time for a few munchies before you start. I'll have Athnasius take you down. I'd do it myself, but I've got a job to do right here watching the Nips—ooright with you?"

"It certainly is, Jim," said Mike Stringer. "You've been more than cooperative. We understand completely, and we're grateful for all you've done."

"Believe me, mates," laughed Jollymore, glancing at Markowski, "the ridgy-didge is the pleasure is mine — all mine."

— —

With Jim Jollymore leading the way, Markowski next, and sidearm-bearing Zachary and Mike Stringer close behind, the four worked their way down the precarious trail to the plantation below.

"Now to find your man—'Athnasius' is the name, isn't it?"

"Right on, Mike."

"And how do we do that?"

"We just stand right here on this flat rock and he'll find us. Athnasius keeps an eye peeled on this place — for me, or the Nips, or if it ever comes to that, to both. But, let's hurry him up a bit." The coastwatcher put both small fingers to his lips and let forth an amazingly high, shrill whistle, dropping markedly to a low note at the end.

"Sounds like a bird," said Zachary. "Not out of place at all."

"By cripes, Zach, that's exactly what it's supposed to be — like a yellow and green parrot common to this area."

Shortly, a figure stepped out from behind one of the palms, hand raised in salutation, and approached the group.

It was the same native, the "bushie" they had seen before. Lean, fit, and colorful, this time in a blue laplap, with arm bands that matched and fuzzy-wuzzy hair, he was holding an unusually long machete—a "bolo" in native argot—over one shoulder.

"Gude, Athnasius," said Jollymore. "Yu stap gut?"

"Yes, masta Jim. Mi stap gut."

"Excuse me, Jim," said Mike Stringer, "what's that you said?"

"Aha! So your pidgin isn't any better than your English! How you Seppos converse is beyond me! But, Athnasius and I were just exchanging bushie pleasantries. I said, 'Yu stap gut?' meaning 'How are you?'. And he answered, 'Mi stap gut' or 'I am well' in your lingo.

"You see, Mike, there are hundreds of tribes here in New Guinea—each with their own language. They call them 'Lost Tribes,' and they truly are. Few of them know any of the others and, amazingly, some of them in the interior have never even *seen* a white man! Hundreds of others have seen only one—the local missionary, that is. Even more amazing—and you might find this even more difficult to believe—some don't know even as much solid down-under English as you do! The only way they do— talk to each other that is—is by way of this handy little Pidgin English.

"Let me give you an example. I'll introduce you to Athnasius." He turned to the native man. "Athnasius, mi laik bai yu bungim Jim Stringer, pren Zachary bilong em— na dispela nogut man nem bilong Markowski."

Athnasius glanced warily at Markowski, then smiled, baring large, black, stained teeth—indicating long-standing addiction to the nut of the betel palm. "Mi hamamas long mitim yu."

"Get it?" queried Jollymore. He's pleased to meet you. You see, most Pidgin is quite logical."

"Is it? Beats me," replied Stringer. "In this case, I'll just have to take your word for it."

"Let's try again." Jollymore touched Athnasius' hair. "Wanem sumting dispela?"

Athnasius went along with the byplay. "Dispela em gras bilong het."

Mike Stringer grinned. "I get it this time! 'This fellow is grass belong head.' You're right, Jim, it is logical—some of it, some of the time, that is."

Jollymore glanced around warily. "Now, let's get down to business." He turned to the "bushie". "Athnasius mipela laik yu gait ol tripela go long solwara painim PT bot. Nau—kwiktaim. Orait?" Athnasius nodded his assent. Jollymore turned to the Americans. "Understand?"

Stringer replied, "Sure, Jim, I think. You told him to take us three down to the salt water to meet a PT boat—right?"

"That's the good oil, mate," grinned the Australian. "And I told him to do it *now*—no delay. 'Kwiktaim.'" He indicated his farewell to Stringer and Zachary with handshakes—and a glower for Markowski. "Go with God—and catch you later." He turned to Athnasius, "Gutbai. Bai mi lukim you tumora."

With that, Athnasius beckoned the group to follow, then set out at a fast pace—"Kwiktaim," recalled Stringer.

"You next, Markowski," he signaled. "We'll be right behind—and behave yourself." He patted his 45. "Understand?"

"Yes, Sir—I do now," came the contrite reply.

In gratifying contrast to their earlier hot, sticky, uphill effort, the contingent made reasonably good time going down. No sign of the enemy was encountered—only a brief pause for the partial transpassage of two asps and their losing battle with Athnasius' bolo—then a more delightful hesitation to allow for the crossing of a large, tan and brown, hairy anteater with a young one on her back.

Shortly thereafter came the now familiar billibong, then the steeper final phase of the trail, including the treacherous stretch of rolling rock—again proving the superiority of a pair of well-indurated native feet over mere GI boots.

Their timing was fortuitous, arriving at the rendezvous beach—'nambis' to Athnasius—as planned, just as dusk was closing in.

Mike Stringer put out his hand to bid farewell to Athnasius, but the native demurred. "Nogat. Mi watim."

"As you wish," smiled Stringer, pleased with his rudimentary understanding of Pidgin English.

He turned to their prisoner. "Okay, Markowski, sit down." He indicated a spot just inside the mangroves bordering the beach. "Zachary and I will take turns standing watch—and if you want anything or wish to move for any reason, ask permission. Got it?"

"All right," came the reply.

"Look, Markowski, do you *really* get it? Unless you want to remain in deep trouble, why don't you start by getting used to the idea the answer is 'All right, *Sir!*'"

The sullen sailor nodded again, looked askance at the officer, then mouthed a petulant "Sir."

Stringer shook his head, an exasperated smile on his face. "Let's try once more, Markowski—for what's ahead of you, you need practice. Give me the whole thing this time: It's '*Yes, Sir.*' Now—let's hear it!"

Markowski looked up, attempting a return of the smile, but only achieving a smirk, "Yes, Sir."

"That's better—keep practicing it," said Stringer, turning to the sea. The obscuring curtain of night continued to be drawn, offset only by the repetitious line of surf racing down the shoreline below the ever-brightening mantle of stars above.

The trio waited, restively, but quietly until finally, about two hours later, the tropical silence was broken by the faint, then increasingly discernible watery murmur of an approaching, muffled PT boat.

"Goodbye, Athnasius," said Mike Stringer, putting out his hand for the second time that evening. "And thanks--many thanks."

"Gutbai," returned the widely smiling native, grasping the preferred hand. "Mi laikim yupela."

The motor torpedo boat—*Miss Sing You* again—slowly emerged from the void, coasting up to, then nuzzling the beach—familiarly, thought Stringer. A Jacob's ladder dropped from the bow, and the weary trio climbed aboard: Ensign Stringer first, their prisoner next, then Zachary, who paused near the top of the ladder, leaned forward, and noisily kissed the forecastle.

After a curious scrutiny of Markowski, Boat Captain McCloud grinned at the others. "Welcome aboard, shipmates."

"Believe me," said Stringer, "as Zachary has just attested so eloquently—or is it 'attasted'?—we're more than happy to be home. It's been a long, long day."

8

As the 150 boat pulled off the sand, Andy McCloud put a hand on his exec's arm.

"Two things, Mike: First, 'nice going' on this mission; second, you'd better have a glance at your favorite beach. You've probably—hopefully—seen the last of it."

"You expressed it correctly, Andy. The beach itself— if devoid of Nips—I could easily become fond of; but that 'stroll' up to Jollymore's cokie cockie I won't miss at all."

Miss Sing You cruised quietly out toward its rendezvous with its companion, this time the 143 boat. Mufflers were bypassed, and shortly, the 150 moved up alongside its companion for the night. Andy McCloud picked up the megaphone.

"Paul? Mission accomplished. All went well and Markowski's at his new post—in the day room under guard. But, it's early. No use wasting another night. Let's see what's doing up the coast."

"You're on, Andy. Lead on."

"Mike," said McCloud turning to his executive officer, "go back and explain to Markowski that, if we get into action, we'll need everyone at his battle station—everyone except him, that is. In that event, he's to remain right where he is and do nothing, say nothing." He grinned. "Tell him to just watch the show for a change. He ought to enjoy that—he's wanted it badly enough! And, seriously Mike, if he doesn't agree, we'll handcuff him for the rest of the night. The choice is his."

Mike Stringer returned a few minutes later and said amidst a yawn and mighty stretch, "Okay, Andy. He says he 'won't be a problem'—and by that, he means *anymore*, I assume."

"I'll buy that when I see it," said McCloud, "and now, Mike, I know you've had a tough day—Zachary, too. I want you two to sack out and sleep well—unless we run into some Nips." He smiled. "In that case, General Quarters will be your alarm clock."

The two boats cruised northeastward snuggled up to the reefs, the 143 boat in seaward echelon. But, as it turned out, not for long. It seemed only minutes later when Spark's voice burst from the speaking tube.

"Skipper! Dead ahead! I'm picking up a half a dozen pips. Looks like they're heading our way!"

"Sound General Quarters, Barbell," said McCloud to his quartermaster as he picked up the microphone.

"Alpha Easy: We've picked up what must be some bogies—dead ahead. Change to a port echelon and get ready for action. Open fire when we do."

"Roger, wilco and out."

A haggard Mike Stringer appeared on the bridge. McCloud grinned.

"Good morning, Mike—had a nice night's rest? Bogies dead ahead—six of them, says Sparks. Refreshed enough to take the helm?"

"Sure, Andy. No problem at all."

With Stringer at the wheel, McCloud picked up his binoculars and scanned the sea ahead. A short time later, he called, "Aha! Got them! And it looks like Sparks is right. Five barges—good sized ones—and what looks like some sort of escort vessel in the lead. They're headed this way, all right—inshore a bit. Should be a perfect setup. Now, Mike, I'll take the helm. You direct the fire."

The boat captain took the wheel, pushed the three throttles full ahead while swinging slightly to port to a course directly at the enemy's lead boat.

He picked up the microphone. "Column astern. Alpha Easy!"

The Japanese escort vessel was hardly caught napping. Opening the fire, with the first line of white-hot tracers seemingly pouring into each observer's eyes—but in reality skimming close over the 150 boat. Momentarily, the volume of fire multiplied as the barges joined in the fray—unusually heavily, mused McCloud. They must be tired of losing troops to our boats.

McCloud swung the helm to starboard, bringing the enemy abeam to port, then barked, "Open fire, Mike—and take that escort bastard first!" All guns responded: the forward 37 and 20 millimeters, two midship twin 50-caliber machine guns, then the pumping of the 40 millimeter aft, the most firepower for its tonnage of any vessel in the Navy. Almost immediately, the 143 joined in, doubling the barrage and overwhelming the escort vessel. It burst into smoke and flames and went dead in the water, with several barges piling up astern.

PT fire switched to the barges, taking one after another under heavy, combined firepower, then ceasing as the enemy was left astern.

With the 143 following faithfully, *Miss Sing You* circled back for another pass, this time ignoring the burning escort vessel and the two barges astern and concentrating most of their fire at the three fleeing barges headed shoreward over the protective reefs.

As the three escapees moved out of effective range, McCloud eased the throttles back, virtually laying to in order to finish off the two remaining barges. The intense fusillade of the two boats proved most effective—all enemy fire ceasing, with what was left of the barges joining the escort vessel in settling into the depths.

McCloud picked up the microphone. "Alpha Easy, that's evidently all we can do. We seem okay; how about you?"

"Not sure, Andy. Give me a moment and I'll be back to you."

After a time—longer than expected—the radio came to life.

"Andy, I'm afraid we didn't make out as well as you—we were raked badly. One engine is out of commission and two of our men were hit."

"Sorry, Paul. What can we do to help?"

"Nothing we can't do here—unless you happen to have a pharmacist's mate aboard, that is. I strongly suggest we head for home."

"Roger that. You take the lead. Set the pace and we'll tag along."

McCloud turned to Stringer. "You've checked and all of our men are all right?"

"All seem well, Andy—and you can be proud of your crew. They did a great job."

"How about the bad boy—Markowski?"

"He's something else! When I asked him if he was okay, he said he was, then burst into a big grin and said, 'Man that was swell—beats the hell out of the engine room!'"

"Well, leave him right there in the day room, but have someone with a 45 keep him company. And, while we crawl home behind Paul, you and Zachary can seize the opportunity to finish your sack time."

With *Miss Sing You* trailing, the stricken 143 boat limped down over the substantial swells of the Huon Gulf—an awkward gait for a PT. Nearing their Morobe destination hours later, the early-morning darkness found them threading their way through the peripheral reefs— "more carefully this time time," according to McCloud— then into and across the bay to the winding inlet beyond. An occasional flash of the 143's searchlight ascertained each turn in the channel, bringing them to adjacent berths under the mangroves fringing the operating base.

"What'll we do with Markowski, Andy?" asked Stringer.

"The answer to that rests with the commander now, Mike. But I'm sure it wouldn't be prudent to disturb him at this hour. Set an armed watch the rest of the night, and we'll check with His Nibs in the morning."

"Will do, Andy."

McCloud nodded. "Excuse me now, Mike. I'm going over to see if there is anything we can do to help our friends on the 143 boat, although I see they already have Doc Shipman coming on board."

— —

Shortly after dawn, Andy McCloud walked up the winding path to the headquarters hut. As he neared the top, the first rays of tropical sun bathed the treetops in light, and with it one of the "birds with the pneumatic armpits" pumped over head. Thinking of Stringer's story of Zachary's more basic description, Andy had to grin. What an eloquent start for the new day!

He walked up the few steps to the screened door of the raised hut, raised his hand to knock, but was preempted by the voice of the squadron commander.

"Good morning, McCloud. Come on in. Have you had breakfast?"

"No, Sir, and if that's an invitation, I accept. After a night like this, it sounds great!"

"Then draw up a chair." The commander turned to the rear of the hut and called, "Sanders, make that breakfast for two."

"And now, Andy, tell me about the night. Mission accomplished?"

"Yes, Sir, it was, only there's more to it than that. That's the good part—all of it went well." He went on to relate the story of Stringer and Zachary's trek, the decimation of the Japanese planes, and the retrieval of Markowski.

Sanders brought and served the breakfast for two. One glance and McCloud applauded. "Oh brother: pancakes—and bacon, too! You're going to spoil me, Sanders. And I love it!"

Sanders beamed. "Yessuh, Mr. McCloud. It's mah pleasure."

"And mine as well," said Winters. "Now, Andy, you called what you've told me 'the good part.' Sounds like another case of 'good news, bad news.' Is that correct?"

"Yes, Sir, I'm afraid it is. Following the Markowski business, it seemed early, so we went hunting and ran into the jackpot: an escort vessel and five good-sized barges. We destroyed the escort and sunk two barges for sure; the other three crossed the reefs, and we don't know how much damage they suffered. They made the shore, but I believe we gave them a bad time of it."

"Excellent, Andy. Naturally, you'll be filing an action report as per usual?"

"Yes, Sir, but in it you'll also find the bad news. Their gunfire was unusually heavy—the heaviest we've seen. We went unscathed, but Paul wasn't as lucky. Their port engine was hit and put out of commission—and worse, two of their men were wounded, one quite badly, I'm afraid."

"How badly?"

"We don't know yet. They're in the sick bay and Doc Shipman is tending to them now. I plan to ascertain that right after this breakfast."

"Good idea, and I'll join you in that. Now, tell me about Markowski. How's he acting?"

"We all agree on one thing in his case. Commander— he's an odd one all right. For example, when he asked me what he was being charged with, I told him I didn't know if it would be "absent without leave" or "desertion"—or both."

"That was correct, Andy. We won't know until it's determined at a Captain's Mast, or even later."

"Yes, Sir, I told him at a mast and or a court martial."

"What did he have to say then? Anything at all?"

"Yes, Sir, he sure did. That's when the kid exploded. 'Court martial! Why a court martial?' I told him I believed if the charge was 'desertion,' there wasn't a choice.

'Desertion in time of war' is one of the offenses that *must* be tried by a court martial. That's correct, isn't it, Sir?"

"That's right, Andy. In fact, it must be a *general* court martial. What did he have to say to that?"

"Not a thing. He's shut up like a clam. Haven't heard a peep from him since, except..."

"Except what?"

"Except to say how much he enjoyed the scrap with the barges. Said it was just great being up where he could see and hear the whole show. Seems he was disappointed when it was over. Imagine that. Commander!"

"Yes, I can see he's different. Where is he now?"

"He's still in the dayroom of my boat—under guard, of course."

"Good. Keep him that way until we have an inquiry a bit later. Let's set that for ten-hundred hours, up here. By the way, Andy, I want you there, and Mike Stringer as well."

"Aye aye. Sir. But I wish we could put Markowski in a brig. It's a nuisance having him aboard. It takes a guard, a man we could use for other things, like getting ready for the next patrol or just catching up on some badly needed shut-eye."

"I understand, and of course we'd do it if we had one. But, until we can rig up a brig, you're stuck with him, I'm afraid. After the Inquiry, we'll have the base force take him off your hands until we have the 143 or some other boat going to Kana Kopa. Perhaps you can check on that. And let me know, won't you?"

"Aye aye, Sir. As to Paul's boat, I would guess there's a good chance the repair of that port engine is beyond the capability of our base force here."

"All right, Andy, we'll know that soon. I see you've about finished your meal. Let's see about those injured men; then I'll get ready for that inquiry while you and Paul check up on the repairs to his boat. And, by the way: have him—Paul—join us at 1000 as well."

"Aye aye to all of that. Commander. And thanks for the chow." Andy rose from the table and turned to the officer's steward standing at the galley door. "And you, too, Sanders. That home cooking was delicious—a real special treat."

Sanders was all smiles. "Yessuh, Mr. McCloud. Ah sure am glad you liked it."

9

Under an unusually heavy sky for an equatorial zone in April, the quintet—Boat Captains Andy McCloud and Paul Corbett, Executive Officer Mike Stringer, the prisoner Markowski, and his armed guard, Boatswain's Mate Zachary—filed up the path to the squadron commander's hut, arriving as ordered at 1000. Andy McCloud prepared to knock, but again, his raised hand paused as Lieutenant Commander Winter's voice directed, "Come right in, all of you."

The squadron commander rose from his desk, natty as usual in informal, but well-pressed khakis in contrast to the boat crews who existed without Sanders' valet services.

Commander Winters gestured. "We'll hold this inquiry over there at the table. Markowski, I want you to sit at the far end facing me; Zachary—isn't it?—behind him. You boat officers and Childers man the sides."

The group arranged themselves as ordered: Boat Captains McCloud and Corbett on one side; Executive

Officer Mike Stringer and Yeoman Childers with his notepad and pen on the other.

"All right," said the squadron commander, "this court of inquiry will come to order." He pointed down the table at the accused. "Markowski, I'm told you've been anxious to tell your story—and now, this is your opportunity to do so. Tell us why you left your duty station, stole the carbine and machete, then surreptitiously left the 150 boat while in enemy territory."

All present turned to the accused. Markowski looked down, licked his lips—obviously collecting his thoughts—then cleared his throat and sat erect in his chair.

"Excuse me, Sir, what do you mean syrup..."

"Surreptitiously. It means furtively, stealthily, *sneakily*, Markowski. Understand?"

"Oh—oh yes. Thank you. Sir. But, to tell my story— the whole one—I have to go back, way back to my family. Is that all right?"

The squadron commander studied their charge at some length. "Markowski, you're in serious trouble. And because of it we want to be completely fair with you. In other words, we want you to go ahead with whatever you believe is pertinent in answering our questions, truthfully, fully, honestly. You say you want to tell it—and believe me, we want to hear it and hear it all. Do you understand?"

"Yes Sir, I—I think I do. And, as I said, to do it right, I have to start with my family.

"You see, Sir, my father was a Marine—a career one: Master Sergeant Matthew Markowski. He was in the Philippines when the war started. He fought at Bataan. Then, when it fell, he escaped to Corregidor and joined the fight there until it surrendered. When that happened, they—the Japanese—took him prisoner and made him part of what they call 'The Death March.'"

Markowski hesitated—obviously distraught.

"We're sorry to hear it," said Lieutenant Commander Winters. "We know it was a bad deal for those involved. Did that name they gave it didn't apply in your father's case?"

Markowski hung his head, hesitated, wiped his eyes.

"Yes, Sir, it did. They—the Japanese—they killed him."

An overpowering silence filled the room—so much so that the only discernible sound was from the wind rustling the thatched exterior of the command hut.

Winters looked at the accused in a new light: kindlier, more compassionately.

"Now we *are* sorry. You have our sincere sympathy on that score. But, go ahead with your story. What does that have to do with you leaving the boat?"

Markowski, more confidently now it seemed, straightened up in his chair.

"Everything, Sir. It's the reason I volunteered for PT boats. I wanted to get back at them—the Japs—because of what they did to my dad."

"Yes?" began Winters. "And you were accepted. My question remains the same: What does that have to, do with your subsequent actions up there near Lae?"

"Well, yes Sir, I was accepted all right, but they made me an engineer. During any action, I was down there in that noisy hole—the engine room—where I couldn't even see or hear what was going on up above." Markowski paused.

"And?"

"And what, Sir?"

"Again, what does that have to do with you leaving your assigned station when the boat was in enemy waters but not engaging the enemy—no firing, no action—but simply carrying out an important mission?"

"Well, Sir, first, as I said, I wanted to get revenge for what they did to my dad. I—I wanted to kill some Japs."

"You said 'first'—there's something else?"

"Oh, yes, Sir: I really wasn't doing anything important down there in the engine room. Pop—Murphy was in charge of the engine room. He was handling all the controls."

"You mean Murphy was sitting in that control seat on the starboard engine, watching the instrument panel, reacting to orders from the bridge, and you were just standing by to assist him as needed?"

"Yes, Sir, that's right. I wasn't doing anything—nothing important, that is. As usual, I might just as well not have been there—and—and this was my first opportunity to do something about it."

"Is that right? So, what *did* you do?"

"Well, Sir, I went topside, then down to Captain McCloud's quarters and...and..."

Andy McCloud finished the statement: "And stole my carbine and its ammunition, then picked up one of the boat's machetes?"

Markowski looked at his boat captain warily. "Ah, yes, Sir—although I don't like the word 'stole.'"

"What word would you suggest?"

"'Borrowed' would be better, Sir."

"Borrowed, eh? And when did you intend to return them?"

"I...I guess I hadn't figured that out yet, but I did intend to do it, Sir."

Lieutenant Commander Winters cleared his throat, then resumed control of the interrogation. "And after you 'stole' or 'borrowed' these weapons, what did you do?"

"Well, then Sir—when everyone was busy on the starboard bow with that Aussie, Mister Jollymore—I slipped off the port stern, waded away from the boat, and went up into the jungle."

Winters' hand gave him pause. "Hold it right there. I don't quite understand. You had never been in that area until that time, had you?"

Markowski shook his head. "No, Sir."

"Yet you said, 'you went up into the jungle.' If so, how did you ever find Jollymore's hideaway? I understand that is anything but easy."

"Well, Sir, when he and his friend—the big native—went up the trail, I followed them."

"So, you knew where to find them when you were tired of hunting Japs?"

"Yes, Sir, something like that. It wasn't easy, but I finally figured it out."

"Now tell us, did you get what you wanted? Did you kill any Japanese?"

"Yes Sir, I did—a few."

"Just a few?"

"Yes Sir. It wasn't easy. They're tough!'

"I see. And did you know that one of the times you went to Jollymore's plantation, the Japs followed you? And when they lost track of you, they questioned two of the natives and killed one of them?"

"No, Sir. I didn't know it at the time, but, later on, Mister Jollymore told me about it. I...I'm real sorry it happened."

"You're serious? Seriously sorry it happened?"

"Yes, Sir—I really am."

Lieutenant Commander Winters studied the accused, then shook his head uncomprehendingly.

"You say you're sorry about leading the Japanese to the native they killed, yet when Jollymore told you it showed why you should stop coming to his hideaway, you continued to do so. How do you explain that?"

Markowski looked confused. "I...I don't know. Sir— except sometimes I needed some food and rest real bad, and someone to talk to I guess. And I...I didn't know anyone else up there."

The commander nodded. "I see, I see, but that doesn't mean I agree with your 'logic.' Tell us, Markowski, do you have anything more to add to what you've told us?"

"No, Sir, I guess that's all of it, except maybe..."

"Except what?"

"Except to say I'm sorry I caused all this trouble."

"It's a bit late to come to that conclusion, Markowski. Now, Zachary, I'd like you to take Markowski outside— out of earshot while I confer with the others here."

With the accused out of the room, the squadron commander turned to his three boat officers.

"This is a weird one, isn't it? Obviously, Markowski thought the world of his father—and, to some extent, I can sympathize with his desire to avenge his death. But, leaving his post and becoming a one-man army is a most unusual way of accomplishing it, and hardly in accord with Navy regulations." Pondering, he rubbed his chin. "At this point, I'm not quite sure what to recommend. What should it be: absent without leave, or desertion—or something else? Do any of you have an opinion you'd like to express before I send him and the result of this inquiry, along with my recommendations, on down to Captain Mooney?"

Lieutenant Paul Corbett raised a hand. "I do, Commander. Markowski said he believed he could leave with impunity because he wasn't needed in the engine room since Murphy was doing all the work. That's plain nonsense. Sir. His job *was* important.

"Just equate that with what happened a bit later in my boat. My lead engineer, McBride, was in that position—in the control seat—and when we mixed it up with those barges, he was knocked out of action by an enemy bullet. Nobody topside knew it, and if we hadn't had an assistant motormac standing by, there wouldn't have been any one to answer signals from the bridge. Why, Sir, we would have been completely out of control!"

The squadron commander nodded. "Good point, Paul." He turned to his other boat captain. "What's your opinion, Andy?"

"First, I agree with Paul. I don't believe Markowski's main fault was running off to take on the Japanese army on his own in order to avenge his father's treatment at their hands—that was just youthful stupidity. The most important point as far as I'm concerned is that he left his assigned post without permission. To me that's plain and simple desertion—desertion in time of war."

Commander Winters nodded, turning to Stringer. "Anything to add, Mike?"

"Not really. Commander. I concur with my boss," he glanced at McCloud and grinned, "like a good executive officer should."

The commander slapped the table. "All right, gentlemen, your opinions are impressive—reasonable and appreciated. Now, let's have Zachary bring our bad boy back in here."

With all present and reseated. Commander Winters pointed at the prisoner.

"Markowski, you are going to be sent down to Kana Kopa—as soon as possible. Captain Mooney, Commodore of PT's New Guinea will consider your case further at a captain's mast. For his use and guidance at that session, he'll have the minutes of this inquiry with my recommendation that your actions be further considered at a court-martial—general perhaps, but summary as a minimum. Do you understand?"

"I...I think so, Sir, most of it."

"What don't you understand?"

Markowski squirmed in his chair. "Well, Sir, the part about general or summary court-martials."

Squadron commander Winters nodded. "'General' is the most serious, 'Summary' is next. The answer to which of them you'll be given will come as the result of the captain's mast. But you'll have plenty of time to read up on it and hear more about it as well from the counsel you'll undoubtedly be given."

He turned to Corbett. "Paul, I understand Doc Shipman wants your two wounded men sent to the rear base. Tell me: what is the condition of your boat?"

"The base force and our men are patching it up. The hull should be okay when they finish today, but one good-sized shell hit the port engine—knocked it to hell and gone. It seems replacing it is too big a job to handle here and, if it's all right with you, we'd like to take her down to the rear base tomorrow."

Commander Winters nodded. "Permission granted, Paul. Take your seriously injured man—or men—and Markowski here as well."

He turned to the prisoner. "You understand, Markowski, you're still under arrest."

Markowski grimaced, even blanched. "Yes Sir, I...I'm afraid I do."

The squadron commander continued. "And, as such, I advise you to be on your best behavior. The final charge could well be 'desertion in time of war'—one of the most serious of all Navy crimes. And, if I were you, I'd be sure not to do anything that would make things worse than they already are.

"Lieutenant McCloud, until tomorrow, put Markowski here in the quonset hut we're going to use as a jury-rigged brig—under guard, of course."

"And Corbett," he said, turning to the other boat captain, "when you get to Kana Kopa, turn Markowski over to Flotilla Commodore Mooney along with the minutes of this inquiry and my recommendations. We'll advise him you're on your way." He looked the group over. "Any questions?"

"No, Sir," the group chorused—except for Markowski.

"Could I ask one, Sir?" he requested.

"Of course, go ahead."

"What is the worst that could happen to me?"

"That all depends on what Captain Mooney advises as a result of his captain's mast—and the subsequent trial in Brisbane, if there is one. As I have said, a general court-martial would be more serious than a summary, and if that turns out to be the decision, a variety of punishments could result—up to and including death."

"Death!" gasped Markowski.

"Easy, son, let me finish. Death *or* such other punishment as the court adjudges, including loss of pay, dishonorable discharge, and/or imprisonment."

"Good Lord—all of that! I didn't know, Sir."

"You didn't know?" The squadron commander turned even more austere. "That's no excuse. The regulations are readily available to all hands, and you in particular—coming from a military family—should have known enough to include a look at them before making those 'carefully laid plans' of yours."

He leaned back and raised a finger. "I'll tell you what we'll do. While you're spending the rest of the day lolling in that brig, we'll furnish you with a copy of Courts and Boards to occupy your time.

"Now, the inquiry is over—you're all dismissed."

10

The following morning, the crippled 143 boat—presciently named *Miss Takeable*—with the two injured men in berths below, and Markowski under guard in the day room amidships, lit off its two viable engines and worked its way down the sinuous inlet, crossing Morobe Bay and this time turning to starboard to begin its impaired cruise down the Papuan tail of the turkey that the contour of New Guinea resembles.

It was a spectacular morning weatherwise—almost clear and bright enough to tempt the unwary into forgetting the war in order to simply enjoy the coastal scenery. First, the boat limped past Cape Ward Hunt. Farther on, it cruised by bloodied Buna with its adjacent airstrip at Dobodura—home base of the planes that had recently decimated the thirty-five ill-fated Japanese arrivals at Lae. Farther on, they approached Mount Victory jutting out to form Cape Nelson with its picturesque Tufi fjord—not long ago the initial advanced base for PT's New Guinea.

Looking up at the cliffs marking the opening to the familiar fjord. Boat Captain Corbett said, "Beautiful as ever, isn't it? I'll never forget standing on that cliff one afternoon—brilliant as this one—admiring the opalescent water down here."

"Right on, Paul," added Jerry Coffey, his executive officer. "And all that opalescence—caused by the reefs you were admiring—is right under us now, with enough water over them to allow us to pass—I hope. With one engine out of commission, the last thing we need is one of your 'opalescent' reefs taking out another one—or, the Good Lord spare us—two of them."

The crippled boat continued its laborious cruise into Goodenough Bay, sitting between Papua to starboard and the D'Entrecasteau Islands to port.

Markowski sat in the dayroom amidships under the watchful eye of Boatswain's Mate Martinac. Martinac, bored, began to complain.

"Boring, isn't it?"

His words had barely left his mouth before they were rebutted by the demanding snarl of the klaxon signalling General Quarters.

"Not anymore it isn't!" he whooped, rising and flinging open the dayroom hatch. "Let's get the hell out of here! I'm manning the port twin fifties!"

Stepping up to the rear of the cockpit, Martinac called, "What's up. Sir?"

Executive Officer Coffey pointed aft. "Turn around. What's up are those Jap planes!"

Their red 'meatballs' glinting in the morning sunshine, three 'Zekes'—Japanese Zero fighters—were winging down and onto the wake of their lone prey: the crippled *Miss Takeable*.

"Man your station, Martinac! And you, Markowski, we're short-handed. We need all the help we can get. Are you willing?"

"*Yes, Sir!* I'd like to!"

"The smoke generator—can you handle it?"

"Yes, Sir—no problem."

"Then aft with you. With this crippled boat, we'll probably need it. Just watch for our signals!"

Boat Captain Corbett picked up the speaking tube to the radioman in the chartroom below. "Stanton, radio the Kana Kopa base that we're being attacked by three Zeros in Goodenough Bay. Understand?"

"Aye aye, Sir, wilco!"

"Prepare to open fire!" bawled Corbett. He turned to his executive officer, now at the crippled boat's helm. "Hard aport, Jerry—now!" Then, back to his megaphone, he ordered, "All guns: Track that lead plane! Ready to open fire—FIRE!"

The four 50-caliber machine guns in turrets amidships and the aft-mounted 40 millimeter Bofors responded in unison. Then, as the planes closed in, the forward 20 millimeter Oerlikon joined in.

The lead pilot—most likely anticipating little resistance from so small a boat, ran slam-bang into the fire from the most heavily armed craft for its size in the Navy and careened hard to port, dipping a wing tip into the sea—ending in a spectacular cartwheel into a watery grave.

"That takes care of one!" cheered Corbett. Then, noting the remaining two Zeros coming around for another pass added, "But it'll only make his buddies more cautious—let's lay smoke!"

He pointed at and gesticulated to Markowski at the smoke generator on the stern. Markowski reacted

89

immediately, cracking the generator—and an instant stream of thick gray smoke poured aft and skyward.

"Keep that smoke between us and the planes. Jerry— and Markowski," he bellowed into the megaphone, "keep it coming!"

An increasingly large and foggy island of smoke continued to build, hanging heavily over the sea astern.

"Jerry! Now throttle down—let's hide out in it— and pray!"

All anxious eyes tried to penetrate the covering screen of smoke—to no avail.

"Hope it's as thick looking down as it is looking up," said Corbett.

After a spell, the boat captain ordered: "Okay, Jerry— let's get out of this smoke and see what's up. Resume your course and speed.

"All hands," he called, "we're coming out of the smoke—be ready to resume fire!"

The PT emerged into the clear, accelerating as much as possible on its two viable engines.

"There, Skipper! There—on the port quarter! There they are!" called Martinac from the vantage point of his 50-caliber turret.

"But look—above and behind them!" McCloud pointed at a welcome sight: five diving, twin-boomed planes—unmistakably American P38 Lightnings.

They were hardly alone in sighting the Lightnings; visibly, so did the enemy. The two remaining Zeros slewed about—soaring northward toward and over the horizon with the P38s in hot and accelerating pursuit.

Boat Captain Corbett smiled broadly. "Thank God for Dick Bong and those new Lightnings. A helluva lot more impressive than those old 39s and 40s, aren't they? And, from what we've just seen, the Nips seem to agree."

"Right on, Skipper," grinned Jerry Coffey. "But, one thing I don't understand—how did they get here so fast?"

"Damned if I know!" He picked up the megaphone again. "All right," he called. "All hands secure from General Quarters. And, Martinac," he said to the boatswain's mate climbing out of the after 50's turret, "bring Markowski up here."

The duo soon appeared at the bridge. "Markowski," said Corbett, "we appreciate your help in this. You did a fine job."

"Thank you, Sir," grinned the prisoner. "I really enjoyed being up here this time!"

"Good," replied Corbett. "Now, Martinac, you and Markowski take up where you left off—in the dayroom."

"But...but Sir," protested Markowski, clearly disappointed. "I thought that...that after what just happened, we might be able to forget all that other stuff and start over."

Corbett turned and leaned over the back of the bridge.

"Markowski, let's get this clear. We appreciate your help today, but that doesn't wash out the fact that you are under arrest and destined for a captain's mast for another matter at another time. I don't know if there is any relationship between the two, but that isn't up to me. I have my orders to deliver you to Captain Mooney at Kana Kopa—and that I intend to do.

"However," he smiled. "I will pass the word along to the Commodore about your assistance today. It can't hurt and may be of some help to you. At least, I hope so."

91

11

Miss Takeable resumed its impaired southeast-
ward trek, finally rounding East Cape—the eastern ex-
tremity of Papua, New Guinea. The islands of Sariba and
Samurai lay to port, Milne Bay to starboard.

Boat Captain Corbett turned to his executive officer.

"Jerry, do you know that island over there—Samurai—was a lively place before the war, famous as one of
the playgrounds for Errol Flynn?"

"The hell you say, Skipper! How about sneaking over
for a look at some of his sexy broads?"

"Sorry, Jerry. I understand it's been tried, but Errol's
long gone—for the duration at least—and so are the girls.
You'll just have to be satisfied with the fuzzy-wuzzies."

"Yeah, Paul, I hope we're not out here that long!"

PT 143 continued its crossing of the mouth of the
Cape, finally idling into Kana Kopa, a cove inside of Milne
Bay's lower lip that had been transformed into the main
PT headquarters and overhaul base for PT's New Guinea.
PT 143 came alongside one of the docks, found an empty

berth, and despite the loss of its port engine, managed to nose in. Boatswain's Mate Martinac stepped off, lines were thrown, the stern pulled in, and the two operable engines secured.

"Jerry," said Corbett, "I'm going to report to Captain Mooney. Wish me luck—I'll probably need it. I've never met the man, but rumor has it that he eats junior lieutenants for breakfast.

"Meanwhile, after you've seen that the injured men are taken care of, get in touch with the overhaul chief and arrange to have us repaired as soon as possible." He pointed at an adjacent boat. "And since they seem to be installing radars, see if we can get on that list as well.

"Meanwhile, keep Markowski under guard where he is until I find out what the Commodore wants to do with him."

Corbett strode down the pier past PT's in various stages of repair: one with a weird-looking piece of armament being installed aft where his boat—the 143—had its 40-millimeter Bofors.

"What in the world is that?" he asked one of the workmen.

"It's a new one—called a 'Thunderbolt,'" was the reply. "As you can see it's a rotating turret with six guns. They say you can track in with these two outboard 50-caliber machine guns, then hit this pedal to actuate the four 20 millimeters."

"Wow!" said Corbett. "That ought to saw an airplane in half—we could have used it earlier this morning!"

The next boat was having a 40 millimeter set in place of its former 20-millimeter Oerlikon, and another getting radar.

"Must be a tremendous asset," mused Corbett.

Reaching the shore, he paused at the first station: a bustling torpedo shop strewn with gear, in the midst of it something new: a shorter, fatter torpedo about 12 or 13 feet long. Putting his hand on its impressively large warhead, he said, "Chief! What is this?"

"That beauty," said the smiling chief petty officer, "is one of the first of our new Mark 13's—the aircraft torpedo they're issuing to the dive bombers. They're not only shorter and more powerful, they're a helluva lot faster—and being lighter, the boat's going to be faster, too. And another real plus, Lieutenant: With these dandies, you can stop worrying that you're going to get one of your own fish up your ass."

"Great! That will be a relief. But, tell me, Chief, how in the world are we going to launch them?" He was referring to the fact that the old, thinner, 21-footers were propelled out of heavy tubes via a black powder charge.

"And that's another real plus," grinned the CPO. "They're made to be dropped from torpedo bombers, so all we have to do is roll them off one of those lightweight racks over there—no flash to tell the Nips 'Hey, better get out of the way. We've just shot a fish at you!' The real plus, I'm told, is that they go where they're aimed!"

"Beautiful! When do we get ours?"

"By any chance are you planning to see the Old Man?"

"That's exactly where I'm heading now."

"Well, why not put in a word for yourself?" The chief torpedoman laughed. "You'd be surprised how pleased I am to do whatever that man suggests!"

Corbett continued upward past the array of shops— carpentry, metal-working, gunnery, electrical—and on further up the trail to the center quonset hut, headquarters of Captain R.C. Mooney, commodore in charge of all motor torpedo boat activity in the New Guinea area. Introducing himself, he asked the yeoman if the captain was available.

"He most certainly is, Lieutenant—and expecting you. Please have a seat."

Corbett wasn't in the seat for long. The commodore himself appeared momentarily. Corbett sprang to attention, and to his surprise, the ogre of rumor smiled disarmingly.

"At ease, Corbett—and come on in." He led the way back into his office, sat down at his desk and motioned Corbett into an adjoining chair.

"Well, well, so you're Paul Corbett. You know, you've been much in our news of late."

"In your news? How so, Captain?"

"Well, first of all, thanks to Commander Winters, we've been expecting you in regard to the man you brought down. Markowski, isn't it?"

"Yes, Sir."

"But, Lieutenant, we didn't anticipate you'd be encountering the Japanese air force on the way."

A more relaxed Corbett returned the smile. "Nor did we, Sir."

"Tell me about it."

"Aye aye. Sir," said Corbett and related his tale of the morning's engagement.

The commodore nodded approvingly. "I see, Corbett. Nice work—particularly with a crippled boat. By the way, we're as surprised as you were that those Nips ventured as far south as they did in broad daylight."

"Yes, Sir—and speaking of surprises, we were surprised that those Lightnings responded so promptly."

"You're welcome, Corbett."

A puzzled Corbett responded, "I beg your pardon, Sir?"

The commodore smiled. "I can understand your bewilderment. You see, we're constantly receiving all radio activity on the pertinent frequencies: ours, the Ferdinand, and the Air Corps. When we heard your problem, we were pleased to find the P38 group in the process of take-off and directed them down to you."

"Oh, now I understand. And believe me. Sir, we're mighty grateful."

"Now you know, Corbett, we're really your guardian angels. Let's hope the lesson the Nips learned about the new Lightnings will prevent any further incursions.

"And, Corbett, speaking of your experience today, congratulations on the new hash mark for your boat."

"The new hash mark. Sir?"

"Why, yes—for that Nip who got his comeuppance."

"Frankly, Sir, we've been wondering about that. But to be completely honest, I'm not sure we deserve it—the hash mark, that is. I don't know if it was the result of our fire or that fellow's slipshod aerobatics—or both."

"Mmmmm," smiled the commodore. "'Slipshod'— that's an inspired word for what happened, isn't it?"

"Yes, Sir—slipped a wing into the water, he did."

"Well, Corbett, let's not belabor the point. Just take the credit while I'm in a generous mood."

"Commander, if I may take full advantage of that 'generous mood,' what I'd really like is to trade the hash mark for something more useful."

"And what might that be, Corbett?"

"A set of those new Mark 13 torpedoes." He hesitated. "Am I being presumptuous, Sir?"

"Well...ahem...yes you are, but in this case I'll over-look it and grant the request. The new torpedoes *and* the hash mark. I will, that is, in exchange for your promise."

" And what promise is that, Sir?"

"Your promise that you'll spread the word that I'm really a decent fellow and an easy mark—not the tough old bastard rumor says I am.

Pausing momentarily to think over the assignment, Corbett grinned broadly.

"You have my pledge on that, Sir. And thank you, Captain. The crew will be more than pleased. "But, Sir, before I leave, I should emphasize Markowski's comport-ment today. Since we had two injured men aboard, we were short-handed when those planes attacked us. We badly needed someone to man the smoke generator. And, Captain, Markowski did it—did a good job, will-ingly—even gleefully. Does that change anything as far as he's concerned?"

"No," frowned the commodore, "not at this point. Just include it in the material for my consideration—and the court's, if it goes that far. But, tell me, Corbett, how is he—Markowski, that is? What is his general attitude?"

The commodore was interrupted by a flash of nearby lightning, followed immediately by a burst of thunder and heavy rain splattering on the quonset roof. The newly amiable commodore smiled.

"Seems like Nature's answer to my question, doesn't it? What's yours, Corbett?"

The boat captain grinned in return. "Well, Sir, 'be-wildered' would be a pretty fair description for it. I'd say he's a mixed-up kid at this point. A fine one in many ways, but 'scatterbrained' —no, that isn't fair—'immature and confused' would be a better description. And,

Commodore, he's yearning to talk—explain his side of the story—and although it doesn't excuse what he did, it is mitigative and well worth hearing. I'm sure you'll find it of interest."

The commodore smiled again. "Hmmm, 'mitigative'—fine word that. Very impressive for a young man who didn't even go to the Naval Academy! But, seriously, as an answer to your recommendation, we will see that he gets that opportunity. Along that line, I must admit to an unusual sense of curiosity about this case, Corbett. From the little I know about it at this point, it seems quite a departure from the norm. And, if I concur with what I understand are Commander Winters' recommendations, the young man is very likely destined for an all-expense-paid trip to Australia for a court-martial.

"And speaking of those recommendations, I understand you have been charged with bringing them to me. Is that correct?"

"Yes Sir, it is—and here they are."

Captain Mooney leafed through the material. "This all seems to be in order. We'll be sending it down to 7th Fleet headquarters as an addendum to my own report. In addition, I suggest you submit whatever comments you care to make regarding his conduct this morning for consideration at the time of the mast—and the subsequent court-martial, if it comes to that. My yeoman, Berger over there, is at your service."

"Thank you, Sir. If it's all right with you, I'm prepared to do that right now."

"Go right ahead," replied the commodore, glancing out of the window at the calmed skies and ending the exchange on an equally benign note. "And, with an extension of the good luck you've had today, by the time you finish, the rain will have stopped."

Paul Corbett pondered the events of the morning—particularly Markowski's conduct. Deciding that, for the upcoming trial—or trials—the facts were needed, not his interpretation of them, he turned to the waiting yeoman. "Well, Berger, I'd like to give you this story while it's fresh in my mind. Ready for it?"

"Yes, Sir. If you don't mind me being personal, it sounds interesting. I'm all set."

McCloud began his narrative, finding Yeoman Berger highly facile, as expected from an employee of the commodore. In the midst of it, the commodore himself reappeared, report in hand.

"I've just been giving this a more thorough look, Corbett, and I find it a bit inadequate—it needs more authority."

"I don't understand, Captain. In what way?"

Commodore Mooney tapped the deposition. "This is all very fine—as far as it goes, that is. But a major portion of the case is secondhand. It's chiefly based on the observations of this coastwatcher, the fellow with the happy name...'

"Oh," grinned Corbett, "'Jollymore'?"

"That's the one. All very interesting, and highly pertinent to the case, but mostly hearsay. What is needed to give it authority is his direct testimony."

"That might prove difficult, Captain. He's importantly involved in the jungle overlooking Lae."

"Yes, I'm well aware of that. Second best, would be his personal deposition. Of course, being an Australian, we can't order him to testify. Tell me: In your opinion, do you think he'd be willing to cooperate with us?"

Paul Corbett laughed. "Captain, I've never met the man, but from what I've been told, that won't be a problem. We should find him delighted to cooperate—after all, he's the one who asked us to get Markowski out of his hair. The only difficulty might be reaching him. As you know, he's hiding away in the hills overlooking Lae, and I understand getting to him takes a bit of time—and effort, too."

The commodore cleared his throat. "Corbett, we've got those—time and effort—to spare. After all, 'desertion in time of war'—if that is the charge—is an extremely severe offense. We can submit no less than fully complete staff work. Consequently—"

"Excuse me, Sir," broke in Corbett, then realizing his presumptuousness, said, "I didn't mean to—"

"It's all right—in this case, that is, Corbett," smiled the commodore. "What is it?"

"It's just that I believe there's another alternative. The former coastwatcher, the one Jollymore relieved—a fellow named Jerry Donegal—saw as much of Markowski as Jollymore did. Since he's available, why not have him testify?"

"Your suggestion is a good one, Corbett, and germane, but I believe there's a major problem with it. As I understand it, Donegal was relieved because he'd been in the tropics too long—long enough to have his judgment questioned. I'm quite certain an alert defense counsel would seize on that to negate his testimony. No, I think we should go directly to Jollymore."

"Yes, Sir, I understand."

"I'll tell Commander Winters to arrange it. Meanwhile, we can't send Markowski to Brisbane with a deficient report—assuming that is the result of the mast, that is. That means holding him here until we complete the case properly, which will take some days, I'm sure. By the way, where is Markowski now?"

"In the dayroom of my boat, Sir—under guard, of course."

"We have a spare quonset we use as a brig. Tell Commander Huey, our base commander, to put Markowski in it—again, under guard. You'll find Huey in the hut next door."

"Aye aye, Sir."

The commodore turned to leave, then cast a final remark over his shoulder.

"By the way, Corbett, that luck of yours is holding. The rain has stopped."

12

Back at the Morobe forward base, Lieutenant Commander Winters entered the radio shack.

"Sparks, in line with that message you gave me from Captain Mooney, can you put me in touch with the Australian Coastwatcher's channel?"

"Yes, Sir, that's an easy one," said the radioman on duty. "As usual, we've been monitoring it. They call it the Ferdinand channel" He turned to his set, listened a bit, then handed the microphone to the squadron commander. "Here you are, Sir. It's ready to go."

"Before I do, Sparks, how do I address Jollymore?"

"Just use the first part, Sir. On the air, he's dropped the 'ex-Don' bit. It's now simply 'Jolly.'"

"Fine, Sparks." He turned back to the microphone.

"This is for Jolly. Winters here. Do you read?"

"Aye, Commander. I read."

"Sorry to bother you, but you are going to have visitors. They will be at your, ah, your cockie tomorrow. Same time, same fellows. Will appreciate your cooperation."

"Aye, mate. Understood."

Winters left the radio shack, glanced up at the threatening sky, then assuming any rain would hold off until late afternoon as usual in these tropics, resumed walking down the trail to the fueling dock, where he turned downstream until he came to the 150 boat. Looking up from the forward 37 millimeter he had been stripping, a startled gunner's mate stood, snapped to attention and saluted.

"Good morning, Commander."

Winters returned the salute. "At ease. Guns. Is your skipper aboard?"

"He is, Commander. I'll get him for you."

The gunner's mate strode aft, rounding the cockpit surround and disappearing down the ladder to the officers' country below. McCloud appeared momentarily.

"Good morning, Commander. Won't you come aboard?"

"Morning, McCloud. I'll just do that. I'd like a chat with you and whoever went up to Jollymore's base— Stringer, wasn't it?"

"That's right, Sir. Mike Stringer and Bosun's Mate Zachary."

"Are they both available?"

"That they are, Sir. But it will take a bit of time. At my suggestion, they're sacked out."

"Most understandable, McCloud. But I'm afraid we're going to have to disturb them. We must have someone go up to the cockie again, and I assume they would be the proper choice?"

"Yes, Sir," grinned McCloud, "they're the ideal pair."

"Have them both join us—in the chartroom if it's clear," said the commander, returning a wisp of a smile.

When Stringer and Zachary arrived—both a bit bleary-eyed—Commander Winters outlined the need for Jollymore's deposition.

"First, however, I want you to ask him if he'd be willing to appear at the commodore's mast, which I'm quite sure he'll turn down—and should. In that case, I want you to get his deposition." The commander went on to describe what the contents of the deposition should be: the story of Markowski's occasional appearance despite Jollymore's protests, the killing of the native by the Japanese who were trailing Markowski, and whatever else Jollymore would like to add. When completed, the document was to be signed and witnessed. "Can you take care of that tonight and tomorrow?"

"Sure, Commander," grinned McCloud, glancing at Mike Stringer. "We can do that—*easily*, can't *we*, Mike? You and Zachary would be delighted to have another stroll up that petite hill, wouldn't you? It should be a breeze the second time—and, after all, you'll only be toting a pen and paper."

"Yes, Sir." Executive Officer Stringer returned the grin. "Of course, it will give us immense pleasure to make your day—and our night, too."

"Fine," smiled the squadron commander. "Then, it's all set?"

"Yes, Sir," said McCloud. "We'll put these two ashore tonight. They can go up and meet Jollymore at the plantation in the morning. Then we'll pick them up tomorrow night and you'll have the deposition the morning after. Will that do the job?"

"That's all I can ask. And, good luck, fellows."

— —

The following morning, Coastwatcher Jollymore and his native colleague Athnasius stepped out of the plantation brush, breaking out in wide, toothy smiles— Jollymore's white and Athnasius's black attesting to the latter's betel nut habit.

Jollymore extended both arms in a welcoming gesture.

"Well, strike us lucky—here you are. Knowing you as lively chaps, we thought you might be coming along about this time."

Tired and disheveled as they were from the arduous trek, the two Americans responded with matching grins.

"Jim," said Mike Stringer, "are we pleased to see you! But, we missed you, as we did most of the asps on the trail." He wiped his brow. "And speaking of that trail, Zach and I agree it's longer and steeper than it was a week ago!"

"Aha, so that's why you look like a pair of stunned mullets. Your tongues are hanging out!"

"If you mean we look a mite thirsty, you're dead right. It's been a long haul from that...that..."

"'Billibong's' the word. You two have earned a reward—after a bit more work. Let's jog up to my place. Just one more little jaunt and we'll wet your whistles. Athnasius, lukaim you bihain."

The trio wound their way up the familiar, but no less torturous path to Jollymore's refuge—"a perfect ninth-inning end to our morning game," according to Zachary.

After struggling up to Jollymore's cave and settling on reasonably conforming rocks with drinks in hand, Mike Stringer outlined the reason for their visit. He told of Markowski's progression through inquiry and captain's mast and, quite likely, a further move on down to Brisbane for a court-martial.

"And for that highly serious session, your testimony is considered vital, Jim. We have two options. The very best one would be for you to come back with us and fly down to Brisbane to tell your story in person."

Jollymore shook his head. "That's a bummer. Eric Feldt would think my tide's gone out for sure."

Stringer grinned and nodded. "We figured that would be your reaction. In that case, we can proceed with the second option: take your deposition."

"My deposition?"

"Sure, Jim, you tell us your story and we put it down on paper. Then, if you agree with our version of it, you sign it and we do the same, as witnesses. That is your preference, isn't it?"

"No, mate, if I can put words in my own mouth, my preference would be the first one — I'd go to Brisbane and get two jobs done. First that testimony bit, and then the bonzer one: a short session with a cooperative Matilda I know down there. But, for Eric's continued mental stability, let's go that deposition route."

Mike Stringer grinned and nodded, taking notepad and pen in hand.

"We understand, Jim. That's a tough choice to have to make. So, here we go. We want your formal relation of events up to, and including, your request that Markowski be removed from the area in order not to spook your mission."

"'Spook my mission?' I suppose that's Septic for not wanting the Nips to know where I am, and what I'm doing?"

Stringer assented. "That, friend Jim, is exactly what we mean. Now, if you'll tell us—nice and slow, since my shorthand is nonexistent—why you requested Markowski's removal from this area, I'll take it down. Then, if you approve of what I've written, all we'll need from you is your signature. We'll add ours, attesting to its validity."

— —

With the deposition complete, approved by Jollymore and witnessed by the two Americans, Mike Stringer and Zachary followed the coastwatcher back down to the plantation—the 'cokie corkie' in Jollymore's patois.

"Why 'cokie corkie'?" queried Stringer.

"Oh, get away with you, mate" was the reply. "As I explained to your boss, in classical English, a 'corkie' is a small landholding—like 'cane corkie' or 'wheat corkie'—"

"Or in this case," blurted Zachary, "a 'cokie corkie'?"

"Starve the lizards," laughed Jollymore. "You Seppos are all the same: consistent, but silly as two-bob watches. But, oho! Here's your guide now. Athnasius, go pas long ot man nambis—wankain hap."

"I give up," said Stringer. "What was that?"

"Oh, I just told him to lead you two men down to the beach—the same place we used before."

"Thank you, Jim. Your hospitality is much appreciated, but it's not necessary to send Athnasius with us. We found our way up here, so I'm sure we can find our way back down."

"No, no—none of that, mate. You're carrying that...that deposition I signed. If the Nips laid an eye on it, I and this operation would be down the gurgler. We just can't take a chance on having this buggered up, so Athnasius will lead you down." He waved in a half-salute. "Hooroo, mates—and God speed."

Mike Stringer put a hand out to the slightly built Australian, and was met by a surprisingly strong grasp in return.

"Goodbye to you, Jim. And thanks—thanks for all you've done for us, and, no doubt, *will* be doing."

With Athnasius in the lead, Stringer next, and Zachary bringing up the rear, the trio began their downward trek, zigzagging through the closely entangled brush. Not much of a trail, thought Stringer, but it's looking much friendlier going down, than that earlier, arduous uphill struggle.

The relatively easy descent gave the Americans time to look around—and the opulence of the surrounding area made it worthwhile. Ferns, flowers, and a myriad variety of colorful trees abounded, equaled only by the super-abundance of birds, butterflies, moths—as well as pesky flies and gnats. Creatures were numerous, too: rats, hanging bats, green lizards, snakes, bandicoots—even a much larger version in the form of another parade-footed, long-haired, spiny anteater.

"Damned if this isn't enjoyable," called Zachary. "Now it's really a 'walk in the park'!"

Athnasius turned finger to lips, the other hand raised in a cautionary gesture, effectively putting a halt to further conversation. From then on, only an occasional swish of Athnasius' bolo shortening the career of a luckless asp interrupted the rest of the trip to the billibong.

After a brief pause to quench their thirsts, the trio resumed their file down the trail—but with their progress considerably slowed as they traversed the steeper, more convoluted and rockier portion down toward their rendezvous shore. In this more unstable section, bare-footed Athnasius strode on with seeming ease—putting the GI-booted progress of his companions to shame. As they neared the shore, the sun faded and a mist began to form, followed by a light evening rain—a common late day occurrence in this tropical zone. After a brief wait in the mangrove-fringed edge of the "nambis," Boatswain's Mate Zachary tapped his watch.

"This is all we need: they're already three minutes late. And the later they are, the wetter we get. Terrible!" he complained in mock anger.

Athnasius raised his hand in a bush gesture, undoubtedly the equivalent of the more familiar "pipe down."

Ensign Stringer checked his own watch, then whispered.

"You're absolutely right, Zach, but—here they come! We'll just have to raise hell with the skipper over such inexcusable tardiness. Would you like to take care of that?"

Zachary grinned in return. "No, Sir. If you don't mind, I'll bow to your superior eloquence—and rank."

Knowing the now familiar ideal conditions of surf and shore, the 150 boat coasted confidently up to the beach. As the cutwater slid up onto the sand, the trio left the mangroves and, with waves of welcome in sight, started down the beach. At midpoint, the evening tranquility was shattered by gunfire. Stringer, in the lead, stiffened, his head snapped back, then collapsed into the sand.

Miss Sing You's twin 50-calibers, the bow 37 and 20 millimeters, followed by the after 40 millimeter Bofors, retaliated, pouring streams of lead left and right—soon eliminating every vestige of enemy action.

Athnasius stooped, gathering the stricken executive officer in his arms. He and Zachary strode down the beach to be met by deeply concerned crew members on the boat's bow. With a concerted effort, the wounded, bloody and moaning but now insensible officer was passed up to the forecastle.

Boat Captain McCloud peered down to those on the beach. "All of you, get aboard! On the double—NOW!"

Athnasius put up a hand. "Bai mi go. Gutbai."

"No, no—we can't leave you here with those Japs! Come with us! Get him aboard, men!"

With guns at the ready and training ashore, the PT backed off the beach, slewed about and, with mufflers now off, roared seaward with Quartermaster Coffey at the helm.

Boat Captain McCloud secured the boat from general quarters, then swung down to the executive officer's cabin, joining Zachary—now in his new role as acting pharmacist's mate, or the closest to it in training aboard the boat.

"How is he, Zach?"

Zachary shook his head. "Not good, I'm afraid. Sir. I only wish I had more experience in this sort of thing! He took two bullets: one that appears to be fairly minor here in the upper arm, but the other—the really serious one— is here in the chest, high in the side."

"What can we do for him?"

Zachary looked up—obviously anguished and eyes moist.

"Very little, I'm afraid, Captain, unless you have some suggestions. All I know *I* can do is just staunch the blood and keep pressure on the wounds—especially the chest— and hope we can get him back to Doc Shipman as quickly as possible. That, and pray, Sir. Pray for a really fine man—man and officer."

"I wish I had some suggestions, Zachary, but I don't, other than what you're doing." Stringer moved slightly, moaning with the effort, but his eyes remained closed. McCloud rose. "Stay with him, Zach. I'll see if we can get you some help."

The 150 boat lost no time in joining the 145 boat, their waiting partner for the night. They slide alongside and the two boat captains conferred.

"Yes, Jim, perhaps we *can* be of some help. Delany, our lead gunner's mate, is pretty handy in that department."

"Well, Mike, send him over. We need all the help we can get." A few minutes later, Delany, first aid kit clutched in one hand, leaped the gap between the boats and was directed down to the stricken officer's quarters below.

With *Miss Sing You* taking the lead, the two boats headed southeast across the Huon Gulf for their Morobe base, emitting a commingled high-pitched roar as throttles were advanced to cruising, then extreme forward to the maximum at flank speed. A calm sea and the cool, moist air proved to be pluses, enhancing the usual pace of something over 40 knots, close to 50 land miles an hour.

On the bridge, McCloud studied Athnasius. The native stood outside of but adjacent to the cockpit, one hand on top of the armor shielding, facing forward, teeth black as the night, fuzzy hair streaming aft in the wind—obviously enjoying the new experience.

Suddenly, vivid sheets of purple light streamed aft from every vertical—mast, gun barrels, and even more dramatic, the long whip antenna. Instantly, a changed, unsettled and fearful-appearing Athnasius called out, pointing upward.

"Kapten, Kapten! Wanem stap paia?"

McCloud frowned. "Paia?" Then he brightened. "Oh, I see: 'paia'—'fire'!" And, in a way he's right; it's called 'Saint Elmo's Fire.' But how in the world do I explain it to him—how do I tell him it's an electrical atmospheric discharge sometimes on a moist night like this particularly at high speed? I give up!

Finally, it came to him.

"Don't worry—it's no trouble, Athnasius—God does it sometimes!"

Mouth open in wonder, more so than ever, Athnasius continued to look up at the eerily streaming antenna, then back to McCloud.

"You tok stret, Kapten? Long God? No trabel?"

Watching the obviously apprehensive native, McCloud thought of his own indoctrination with St. Elmo's fire—and decided to try his reassuring best. He beckoned Athnasius closer to the armor's edge, smiled, and behind cupped hand, said: "That's right—'no trabel.' Another thing, Athnasius. My pidgin's nogut—but I'm trying. You savvy English?"

The native, seeing the Saint Elmo's Fire fading, bared his stained teeth in a return smile. "Mi save Inglis liklik. Tok isi plis."

"All right, Athnasius. Stringer needs doctor. You savvy?"

"Mi save, masta. Mi save 'docta.'"

"Good. We go home—to boat home. Doctor is there. Savvy?"

Athnasius nodded pleasantly, apparently pleased with the exchange, then turned sober. "Na wanem time bai mi kam bek?"

It was McCloud's turn to brighten. "Now, I savvy. You go back tomorrow night. Okay?"

"Tengku," smiled Athnasius. "Stap," and he mouthed the next word carefully: "Okay."

With *Miss Sing You* continuing to lead, the two boats continued their torrid pace in the race against time. Andy McCloud checked his watch, then turned the helm over to Quartermaster Coffey and swung down through the chartroom to the officers' country below.

Opening the door to the executive officer's cabin, he paused and surveyed the scene: the recumbent Stringer on the blood-stained bunk, the seated boatswain's mate in an adjacent chair, and Delany kneeling alongside taking the patient's pulse.

"How's he doing, Zachary?"

Zachary shook his head. "I wish we knew. Skipper, but frankly, I don't like what I see. He hasn't regained consciousness and his heartbeat is slow and erratic—it still is, isn't it, Mike?"

Delany nodded. "No change, Zach."

"Anything else?" queried McCloud.

"No, Sir, except we've helped in the bleeding department—externally, at least. I...I only wish Doc Shipman was here."

McCloud nodded. "And in that, you're not alone. We've alerted him to the problem but the only good news is that, at this speed, we should be with him in about an hour and a half."

— —

The two skimming PTs came within sight of Morobe. As they approached the reefs, throttles were pulled back, the boats settled down, and McCloud relieved the quartermaster at the helm of *Miss Sing You.*

"Nothing against your ability, Coffey," said McCloud, "but, under the circumstances, we're not going to creep through these reefs as usual. And, to hell with security! Man the searchlight and find that marker for me."

In response, the bright beam of light pierced the darkness ahead, probed from side to side, then stopped as it centered on the small, elusive white buoy.

"Right on, Coffey. Now, hold it there." McCloud corrected the course to leave the marker close to port. As the boat sped by the buoy, the boat captain ordered, "Secure the light, Coffey. We'll be okay now."

And, this time, they were.

— —

Back at the base early the next morning. Squadron Commander Winters greeted McCloud at the command hut door.

"Good morning, Andy. I was told of your call to Doc Shipman. How is Stringer?"

"Not good at all, I'm afraid, Sir. Doc is doing his level best, but with the limited facilities at hand up here, the outcome of that chest wound is in doubt. Mike has finally regained consciousness—barely and spasmodically, that is—and Doc is patching him up. But as I said, he's limited in what he can do for him. The arm he can take care of, but that chest wound is another matter. The real work will have to be done where facilities are more adequate."

"That's certainly understandable. We'll see what's available in the Milne Bay area and, if necessary, have him flown to Australia. It's a shame. He's a fine, young officer, isn't he?"

"Just excellent, Commander. And, what's more, he's my good and trusted friend. Frankly, Sir, I feel terrible about it."

"And, that too, I can understand. Be assured, McCloud, we intend to do all we can for him. As for you, we have no extra boat officers up here, so we'll have to ask the rear base to ship one up. Meanwhile, we'll just have to borrow one from a non-patrolling boat on a night-by-night basis.

"And another thing. This alters Markowski's case considerably—certainly adds to the severity of it." Winters motioned toward the leather envelope in the boat captain's hand. "By any chance, is that Jollymore's deposition?"

"Yes, Sir, it certainly is. And, as you can see, it's an eloquent testimonial to what happened to Mike. Apparently, he had it under his arm—the one that took the bullet. See? It went through the case, and the deposition as well."

"Really? And what's the condition of it—the deposition, that is?"

McCloud drew it out. "As you can see it's all right—legible even though the bullet put this hole through the margin."

"I see," said the commander, "and your description is most apt. It's 'eloquent,' all right—and, as I said, it's not going to help Markowski's case one bit."

13

Five days after Boat Captain Corbett's session with Captain Mooney, his yeoman, Berger, came down the dock, past other boats in various stages of repair and refitting. He ducked under the boom of the crane that had picked the old 21-foot torpedoes and tubes off the 143 boat and currently was swinging a new Packard Supermarine into its portside position.

Arriving alongside, he called, "Is Lieutenant Corbett aboard?"

"No," replied Boatswain's Mate Martinac, "but I know where to find him. What can I do for you?"

"You can tell him that Captain Mooney is going to hold a mast for the fellow named Markowski at 0900 today and wants Lieutenant Corbett to be present—as well as Markowski and the bosun who served as his guard."

"That 'bosun' part is easy—I'm the guy."

Berger grinned. "That *was* easy. Now, can you get the word to the lieutenant?"

"That I can and will do."

It proved to be a bright and sunny midmorning at the palm-studded Kana Kopa base. As scheduled, the mast participants walked up through the resultant light and shadow, zeroing in on the commodore's central quonset. As they stepped in, Yeoman Berger directed them to an inner conference room. Central to it was a sizeable table and chairs. Berger indicated that the chair at the head of the table was, naturally, reserved for Captain Mooney, suggesting that Lieutenant Corbett and Martinac sit on one side. Berger and Zachary would take the other, and Markowski the chair facing the captain.

After a brief and silent wait, the commodore appeared and all present rose.

"At ease—and be seated," said Captain Mooney. "Now, this mast will come to order. As you know, this mast is in session to go over and expand on Commander Winters' recommendations in the case of the United States versus Motor Machinist's Mate 3rd class Myron Markowski.

Corbett studied Markowski and found a thoroughly frightened and tremulous young man before him.

"The preliminaries of this mast are the same as those in the inquiry held at the advance base. You all were in attendance, so to avoid unnecessary redundancies, I want you, Berger, to make those minutes the initial part of these proceedings—unless I hear objections to it. Are there any?" There were none.

The captain resumed with an initial, resounding "Harrumph!" then continued.

"Now, since you two—Lieutenant Corbett and the accused—were, of course, present at the Morobe inquiry, you know that the hearing revolved around one main issue. That was the question of whether the accused was to be charged with being 'absent without leave' or with 'desertion'—in this instance 'desertion, the United States being in a state of war.'"

"Commander Winters has recommended the latter—the charge of 'desertion'—and, Markowski, after studying the description of your surreptitious departure from the boat, your unofficial pursuit of the enemy, and your persistent interference with the vital work of the coastwatchers, I agree wholeheartedly. If the Commander Seventh Fleet concurs, it means a general court-martial is mandated. Now, are there any questions, or does anyone have anything to add?"

"Yes, Sir," said Corbett, skipper of the 143 boat. "On the way down here, we were taken under fire by Japanese aircraft, and because we had a crippled boat and were short-handed with two of our men injured, we asked Markowski if he would help out, and he did—willingly and capably, I might add. I have given Yeoman Berger a complete account of it and I understand it will be included in the record of this mast."

"That is correct," said the commodore. "Is there anything else?"

After a brief pause, a drawn and white-faced Markowski spoke hesitantly. "Captain, Sir, can...can I say something?"

"Of course. You have every right to do so. Let's hear it."

"Sir, I did what I did because of what they—the Japs—did to my dad. They...they killed him in the Philippines on that Death March, and I wanted to kill some of them because of what they did to him. But, Sir, I was told I

would have some help, a con...counsel, they said, to help
me with my story—and I don't have one."

"I understand, young man, and of course you have
that right. But, since I agree with Commander Winters
that this is a case of desertion in time of war, my recommendation is going to be that the trial must be a general
court-martial—and if and when it is, you most certainly
will have the services of a counsel. You, however, should
feel free to speak in your own behalf at any time—now,
and/or at the trial itself. Do you understand?"

"I...I think so. Sir."

"You think so? Do you have any problem with it?"

"N...no, I don't think so, Sir."

"All right, then," resumed the commodore, "we'll
leave it at that. Speak up at any time. Now, as I said
formerly, I agree with Commander Winters' recommendation that the charge should be 'desertion' and, of course,
it goes without saying that it is 'in time of war.'

"Further, I also agree with the fact that this particular
desertion not only is a case of leaving a duty post under
general quarters conditions, but in doing so, it imperiled
the important clandestine mission—if not the very lives—
of the Allied coastwatchers. That is spelled out in a deposition obtained from Mr. Jollymore—one of the
coastwatchers involved—a few days ago. That deposition is here for anyone to read. You will find it not only
factual, but with no surprises. It will accompany the pertinent material we will be sending to Brisbane."

Captian Mooney paused. "Perhaps I should amend my
reference to 'no surprises.' It should be part of the record
that Jollymore's deposition was taken by witnesses Ensign Stringer and Boatswain's Mate Zachary a few days
ago. Unfortunately, in obtaining it, it seems the enemy

had been alerted to our recent activity in the area and Stringer, Zachary here, and a native associate of Jollymore's were taken under fire at the beachhead. Ensign Stringer was seriously—hopefully, not fatally—injured. Are you aware of that, Markowski?"

"Y...Yes, I know, Sir, and I feel terrible!" cried an obviously anguished Markowski. "How is he, Sir?"

"He's here as you probably know, and our doctors describe his condition as 'critical.' In other words, we don't know the outcome at this point."

With a sob, Markowski buried his face in his hands.

Paul Corbett, noting the genuine sympathy with which Captain Mooney was watching Markowski's heaving back, knew that if the scene could have had broad circulation throughout the flotilla, the commodore's reputation as a hard-nosed son-of-a-bitch would be considerably eroded—if not erased in its entirety.

The commodore cleared his throat loudly. "Now, unless anyone present has anything to add, I conclude this mast in concurrence with Commander Winters' recommendation that, subject to Admiral Woodstock's approval, the accused will be transported to Brisbane to stand trial at a general court-martial for 'desertion, the United States being in a state of war.'"

Captain Mooney surveyed those present. No one spoke.

"So be it."

14

The well-worn Army Air Corps C47—colorfully worn up to a point including bullet holes patched with interior band-aids—carried equipment requiring repair, plus a hodgepodge of passengers—Army mostly, but including two nurses, a few civilians, Markowski and his armed guard, and, to their awe and consternation, a richly beribboned major general.

The plane droned southward with the seemingly preoccupied general gazing unremittingly out of the port-hole-sized window. Finally, as the venerable plane neared the Australian coast near Cairns, the general turned from the window, and noting the others watching him, he spoke.

"I suppose you're wondering why I've been staring at that wing all this time. Well, I want you young people to know I've been part of this man's Air Force since the mid-twenties—and, try as I might, I'm still trying to figure out what keeps the damned thing up!"

A few hours later, the plane made a screeching touchdown on the Brisbane airstrip, searched for, found, and rolled to a stop on the apron in front of a yawning military hangar.

The flight attendant opened the door and lowered the ladder to a cool, somewhat cloudy day—a striking contrast to the equatorial heat of New Guinea. The passengers deferred to the general, who was saluted to the deck by several lower-ranking officers. The rest then clambered off, leaving Markowski and his guard to the last, who were met by two shore patrol sailors wearing striking rarities to the islands duo: well-pressed uniforms and MP armbands.

"You're Markowski, I assume?" asked one, a burly, scowling gunner's mate, first class.

"Yeah, that's me," said the prisoner. "Where are we going?"

"*We* are going to the USS *Bay City*—a nice new, large submarine tender at the New Farm Wharf. *You* are going to be one of the first to try her palatial brig for size."

"Large" was no exaggeration. When Markowski and the two military police arrived at the dock, they got out of the jeep and looked up, left to right, from bow to stern at the immaculate, gray hull of the new sub tender. With a mind accustomed to 80-foot PT's, the *Bay City* looked enormous—close to endless.

"Up you go," said the lead MP pointing toward the guarded gangway.

— —

"Atten—SHUN!" barked the chief petty officer in charge of the brig. Markowski rolled out of his bunk, coming to his feet to face two well-groomed officers in beribboned khakis, one with a "scrambled eggs" encrusted visor—all jarringly impressive to the lone, young, third-class motor machinist's mate.

The senior officer—a four-striped captain—spoke resoundingly with a voice as starched as his uniform,

"So you're the infamous Markowski."

"Yes...yes, Sir, I'm Markowski, but I don't know about...about...what did you call me, Sir? 'Infamous'?"

"Don't get me wrong, young man. I'm not leaping to its use in a derogatory sense—perhaps 'notorious' would be a better term. I believe, at this point, those who are acquainted with it would agree that yours is a unique case--one attracting unusual attention down here.

"But, first let me start with an introduction. Admiral Woodstock has endorsed your trial for 'desertion in time of war.' That, young man, is a highly serious general court-martial charge.

"Seven officers have been named as members of the court, and I, as the senior member, has been named its president. I am Captain Marshall O'Brien, a member of JAG. You're familiar with it, are you not?"

Markowski squinted, wrinkling his brow in thought. "No Sir. I...I think I've heard of it, but I...I don't know what it is."

"Well, you will from now on. 'JAG' stands for 'Judge Advocate General'—the legal arm of the Navy. As I said, seven of us officers have been named to hear your case, and I, as senior member, will preside as both judge and president. That means—divergent to civilian practice— I will serve with the other six on your jury—and as its foreman. Are you with me?"

"Y...yes, Sir, I think so, Sir."

"Good. Your case will be heard as expeditiously as possible. Lieutenant Commander Maxwell Fields has been named judge advocate and, as such, will be representing the United States government as its prosecuting attorney. Still with me?"

"I think so, Sir. That means he's against me, doesn't it?"

"Well, not exactly. He's not supposed to be taking sides—just making the government's case that you are guilty as charged. Do you see the difference?"

"No, not really, Sir."

"Well...ahem...I believe we're picking nits."

"Excuse me, Sir. I don't understand 'picking nits.'"

"'Picking nits?' Why, that's like being overly discriminatory."

"Excuse me again, Sir. Overly discrim...I don't know that either."

"That's the same thing. Making needless ado—being *fussy*, sailor. But, let us go on. To balance it out, and in preparation for the trial, and during the trial itself, you are entitled to legal counsel. Are you with me now?"

"Yes, Sir. I've been told that and I'm anxious to meet with him."

"Fine. Do you have anyone in mind for the job?"

"No...no Sir. I don't know anyone like that."

"In that case, Lieutenant Commander Norman Trimble here is being named to that position. He is a member of the convening authority's—that's Admiral Woodstock—staff. He has had civilian as well as naval legal training and experience—and is well qualified to advise and represent you." The captain smiled. "You might say he's *for* you."

Markowski looked at Commander Trimble appraisingly. He found a fairly short man, pale and rather plump for a Navy officer—in all, not very impressive. Then their eyes met and instantly he became the appraisee.

His impression of his new counsel turned an abrupt 180 degrees.

"That's it for now," said the captain. "Do you have any problem with any of it?"

Markowski glanced nervously from one officer to the other. "Yes, Sir, I do. I've tried to tell my side of the story ever since they arrested me. But, Sir, nobody seemed to give it much time."

"What did they tell you?"

"They all seemed to say the same thing, that I was to be court-martialed, and I could tell my whole story then."

"Well, young man, they were absolutely correct. And now, your time has come. You're about to have that full opportunity. You can discuss the whole matter with your new friend, confidant, and advisor here, Commander Trimble."

With that, Captain O'Brien left the room and Lieutenant Commander Trimble took over.

"Come with me, Markowski. There's a small office nearby where we can talk more comfortably and alone, just the two of us."

"Small" was the correct word for it: small, sparse, but adequate for their purpose. And to Markowski's relief, in contrast to the dark, inner compartment forming the ship's brig, light—blessed light—streamed through a porthole.

Seated, Lieutenant Commander Trimble relaxed visibly.

"All right, Markowski: have a seat and try to make yourself comfortable. And now, just relax and take it easy. Start from the beginning and tell me the whole story. Leave nothing out." He tapped his charge on the knee. "I insist on one proviso, however, an all-important one. In this whole procedure, you must regard me as your close friend and confidant. I'm going to do my best for you and, in return, you must level with me: completely, thoroughly, honestly. Get it?"

"Yes, Sir, I will."

"Now, go ahead with your story. You say you've been wanting to tell it and, believe me, I damned well want to hear it."

15

Markowski's general court-martial convened in a room in one of a series of dockside buildings—this one temporarily loaned to, and flying the ensign of, the United States.

Despite the common warehouse exterior, the interior ambience was surprisingly formal for a temporary military court. As judge and president. Captain O'Brien presided from a table on a raised platform, centrally located near the rear wall with a large American flag as a backdrop. The six other officers comprising the jury—one captain, two commanders, two lieutenant commanders and a Marine Corps captain—sat behind a balustrade on the judge's right; in the forefront, the prosecution and defense were placed at left and right tables; and behind was a large, chaired space for spectators.

A generously windowed wall on the left afforded an impressive view of the spanking new USS *Bay City*. To Markowski—accustomed to the constrained quarters of a PT boat, the ship continued to look tremendous—akin to and symbolic of the forces and charges arrayed against him.

The designated judge advocate, the equivalent of a prosecutor in civilian law—in this case, Lieutenant Commander Maxwell Fields—and a yeoman sat at the prosecution table in the left forefront; Lieutenant Commander Norman Trimble, his yeoman, and Markowski took their places at the defense table on the right. A group of curious, carefully screened onlookers—all military personnel—occupied chairs to the rear.

Looking around the assembly, the obviously nervous defendant murmured, "Good Lord! All this for me!"

His counsel leaned over and whispered, "Take it easy, Markowski. Try to relax—there's nothing unusual here. It's just the way I told you it would be—everything's copacetic."

An unreconciled Markowski glanced at the counsel and grimaced. "That's easy for you to say, you're not—"

"And you're out of order. Calm down, son." He patted his apprehensive charge on the arm and with a slight smile, whispered, "And, that's an order!"

— —

Captain O'Brien rapped his gavel once, then sharply a few more times.

"This Court will come to order!" It did.

Turning to the designated judge advocate and reading from his notes, he directed: "Raise your right hand and repeat after me: I, Lieutenant Commander Maxwell Fields, do affirm that I will keep a true record of the evidence given to and the proceedings of this court; that I will not divulge or by any means disclose the sentence of the court until it shall have been approved by the proper authority; and that I will not at any time divulge or disclose the vote or opinion of any particular member of the court unless required so to do before a court of justice in due course of law." The judge advocate's repetition followed as directed. Captain O'Brien introduced Lieutenant Commander Trimble with a similar, but slightly more constrained oath.

In turn, Judge Advocate Fields gave the routine oath to the members of the Court: "I—your name—do swear that I will truly try without prejudice or partiality the case now pending, according to the evidence which shall come before the court, the Rules for the Government of the Navy, and my own conscience; that I will not by any means divulge or disclose the sentence of the court until it shall have been approved by proper authority; and that I will not at any time divulge or disclose the vote or opinion of any particular member of the court, unless required to do so before a court of justice in due course of law."

Captain O'Brien nodded his approval. "Thank you, Judge Advocate. And now, having gone through the necessary formalities, let us proceed with the case itself. Please read the charge. Commander."

As instructed, Judge Advocate Lieutenant Commander Fields selected the proper papers from his desk, and turning to the court, read:

"Charge Number One: Desertion. While regularly detailed as a member of the crew of PT 150, a unit of commissioned Motor Torpedo Boat Squadron 8, Motor Machinist's Mate Third Class Myron Markowski, on December 16, 1943, willfully, without authority and without justifiable cause, left his assigned post in the engine room of the aforementioned motor torpedo boat and deserted, the United States then being in a state of war.

"Charge Number Two: Theft. The above-mentioned Markowski appropriated certain weapons of government issue to his own purpose while off the boat as described above.

"Charge Number Three: Unauthorized Attacks on Enemy. The above-mentioned Markowski, while in desertion from PT 150, planned and carried out individual and unauthorized attacks on the enemy.

"Charge Number Four: Unauthorized Interference with Allied Coastwatchers. The above-mentioned Markowski, between his personal search for, and attacks on, the enemy, despite pleas to the contrary, intermittently sought out Allied coastwatchers, interfering with and endangering said coastwatchers' mission, if not their very lives."

Judge Advocate Fields put down the papers and picked up a light-blue booklet.

"And now, Mr. President, allow me to read from the 1937 version of Naval Courts and Boards: Offenses Punishable by Death: 'The punishment of death, or such other punishment as a court-martial may adjudge, may be inflicted on any person in the Naval Service: Number 6—who, in time of war, deserts or entices others to desert (the latter part of this 'entices others to desert' not being applicable); Number 7—in time of war, deserts or betrays his trust; and, Number 9—leaves his station before being regularly relieved.'"

Captain O'Brien nodded approvingly. "Thank you, Judge Advocate Fields." He turned to the defense table on his right. "Motor Machinist's Mate Markowski, you have heard the charges. How do you plead?"

Markowski looked startled and bewildered. His counsel, Lieutenant Commander Trimble, leaned over and conferred with him briefly before the young sailor looked up at the Captain and, in a hesitant voice, said, "S...Sir, I plead 'not guilty.'"

"And now," said the Captain, "since Lieutenant Commander Norman Trimble, Counsel for the Defense, has already been introduced, I would like you. Lieutenant Commander Fields, to proceed with your case. Judge Advocate, the deck is yours."

16

To Markowski, Lieutenant Commander Fields seemed the very antithesis of his own counsel: hair a trifle long for a naval officer, hawk-nosed, prominently high cheekbones, slim. He looked cadaverous, hungry, in need of a square meal.

Judge Advocate Fields walked over to the defense table, stood before Markowski, and to the defendent's discomfort, studied him at length before turning to the court.

"Gentlemen, to fully understand the severity of the crime, or crimes, this man is accused of, it is necessary to fully understand the importance of the work of the Australian Coastwatcher System—not only to their homeland, but to our own war effort as well."

Fields turned to address not just the members of the court, but all others in the room as well.

"To everyone in this courtroom, spectators as well as members, let me stress the extreme confidentiality of all references to the system in general, but especially, particular portions of it, such as we find it necessary to do in pursuing this case. Any reference to it outside of these walls would be incalculably dangerous to these extraordinarily courageous people and their vital mission.

"I feel quite certain you are cognizant of the general nature of their program, but in order to be sure we are all of like mind, let me summarize." The judge advocate went on to outline the well-known, prewar expansionist ambitions of the Japanese, the fear that it might endanger or even encompass the northern regions of Australia itself, and, in response, the creation and subsequent enlargement of the coastwatcher system.

"In reality, I am sure the Japanese are well aware of the overall system; it is the particulars essential to the pursuit of this case that *must not* leave the confines of this room."

He turned to Captain O'Brien. "And that, Mr. President, brings up a collateral point. Since, in the prosecution of this case it is going to be necessary to speak of certain particulars of that coastwatcher system, I would recommend that these proceedings not be made public — even to the general military public itself."

President O'Brien leaned forward. "That, Judge Advocate, is understandable, valid, and will be so recommended to the convening authority. And to you observers—all members of the military—I wish to make it clear at the outset that references to these coastwatcher systems outside of this courtroom will be considered chargeable actions."

Commander Fields resumed his dissertation.

"Now, gentlemen of the court—and onlookers as well—let me tell of the actions of the accused while our

New Guinea PT's were assisting in the use and implementation of information from this coastwatcher system."

He went on to tell of Markowski's "desertion," his subsequent pursuit of a single-handed campaign against the Japanese entrenched in the Lae area, and his persistent interference in, and imperilment of, the mission of coastwatchers Donegal and Jollymore.

"Initially, here was PT 150, with its crew at general quarters, in the process of surreptitiously putting a thoroughly trained and experienced relief coastwatcher ashore in enemy-held territory. Instead of remaing at his assigned station in the engine room, the accused left that station, crept into other compartments of the boat—including the officers' quarters—stole a carbine, ammunition, and presumably some rations. Then, while most of the crew was on the starboard bow, concentrating on the official matters of the night, he—the accused—sneaked off the port stern into the water, waded ashore, and crept up into the jungle.

"Subsequently, he covertly followed Jollymore—the relief coastwatcher—and his native companion—up the crag to his hideaway and its nearby secret viewpoints of Japanese traffic in and out of the garrison and air base at Lae. Fortunately, nothing he did at the moment disrupted the coastwatcher mission. Later, however, despite the coastwatchers' pleas and persistent exhortations to the contrary, he did endanger it as he sought repetitive respite from his unauthorized one-man war.

"Certainly, it was not beyond the realm of possibility that these activities of the accused might generate pursuit by the enemy—and, when so engaged, lead them to the coastwatcher's top-secret retreat. As a matter of fact, this is not a matter of conjecture, since one Japanese group *did* attempt to track the accused. Fortunately, they lost his trail in the final portion—but came close enough to encounter and question a native associate of Coastwatcher Jollymore's. Receiving what they considered unsatisfactory answers as to the coastwatcher location, they killed him.

"Gentlemen, imagine what would have happened if they—the Japanese—had been successful in that pursuit! Even more than the inevitable demise of the coastwatcher, the subsequent harm to the Allied war effort in New Guinea would have been substantial—nay, far more than that: nigh unto disasterous.

"Further, and in a way directly related to the actions of the accused, more harm occurred in a later, correlated patrol, this one to gain a deposition from Jollymore considered essential to this trial. This time, unfortunately, the enemy *was* alerted, intervened, and in the consequent exchange of gunfire. Ensign Mike Stringer, executive officer of PT 150 who had secured the subject deposition, was seriously wounded. And, gentlemen, as of this moment, his very survival remains in doubt."

Markowski moaned, head in hands.

"Hush!" said his counsel. "You're hurting your case!"

The judge advocate turned to the bench. "To get back to the coastwatchers, it was our hope to present Jim Jollymore, the current coastwatcher in that area, as a witness to this court, but his preoccupation with his duties made that an unacceptable option. As I mentioned in my reference to the injury to Ensign Stringer, we are planning to compensate for our inability to personally present Coastwatcher Jollymore to this court with a reasonable and, hopefully, effective alternative. But, in order to keep things in their proper sequence, I would like to first call

Lieutenant Junior Grade Andrew McCloud, captain of PT 150."

President of the court Captain O'Brien, bible in hand, administered the oath: "Do you solemnly swear that the evidence you are about to give in the case now before this court shall be the truth, the whole truth, and nothing but the truth, and that you will state everything within your knowledge pertinent to the charges—so help you God?"

Andy McCloud, hand raised, replied. "I do so swear."

Judge Advocate Fields advanced to the witness stand.

"Lieutenant McCloud, you were the skipper of PT 150 the night in question?"

"Yes, Sir, I was."

"And Motor Machinist Mate Markowski was a member of your crew?"

"That is correct."

"Tell the court: At that time, were you aware of the accused's unhappiness with his duties in the engine room?"

"Yes, in a way, but to my knowledge at the time, it wasn't an issue of vital importance to our operations."

"What do you mean by 'in a way'?"

"Well, Sir, because of the limited number of personnel on a motor torpedo boat, PT men and officers are trained to some extent in all other stations and an occasional request to try an alternative one is not unusual. In Markowski's case, we officers weren't aware of any untoward, or unusual, dissatisfaction with his assignment. Although—to be completely fair—we did know he was somewhat displeased by the fact that, in an action, he couldn't see what was going on topside. But, of course, that's the nature of the billet. After all, the reverse is just as true: The men topside can't see what is going on below decks."

Commander Fields nodded. "I see. But to probe a bit further, did you, as his boat captain, have any reason to believe that, in order to compensate for this deficiency, the accused would contemplate going to the lengths he did? That is, to clandestinely leave the boat at the first opportunity in order to carry on a private war with the Japanese?"

"Lord, no! None at the time. As I indicated, we were aware of the fact he would prefer to have a battle station topside at one of the guns, but as was explained to him, his assignment in the engine room was considered equally vital to our missions."

"I see. But you said 'not at the time.' Does that mean you became aware of it later on?"

"Well, yes, but not until his desertion."

"Objection!" called Defense Counsel Trimble. "*Desertion* is the focus of this case. The term has been used before—unfairly employed, that is. After all, that is what this court is attempting to ascertain—and we're a long, long way from that judgment."

"Objection sustained," said President O'Brien. "Please use another term, Lieutenant."

"Sorry, Sir. I understand. I was merely attempting to say it was only after the fact that we became aware that his dissatisfaction with his assignment was so intense that he would contemplate, surreptitiously...ah...'slipping off the boat' in order to carry on his own personal war with the Japanese. It was only in discussing it later with some of the members of the crew—one in particular—that we learned of Markowski's extraordinary hatred of the enemy and his impassioned desire to have a more personal role in—as he was said to have phrased it—'killing them.'"

"Lieutenant, to get back to the night he 'slipped off the boat,' did you have any idea that he planned to make the war so personal an issue as to steal weapons from the boat's issue?"

"Objection!" called Trimble. "Isn't it true that the carbine and ammunition in question was not 'issued' to your boat, but was an unauthorized gift from a Marine officer to you. Lieutenant McCloud, in exchange for a ride on your PT boat?"

"Hold on!" came the rejoinder from the judge advocate. "The carbine and its ammunition was the property of the United States government whether or not it had been specifically 'issued' to the 150 boat."

President O'Brien interceded. "Gentlemen, gentlemen: the court is inclined to side with the prosecution in this matter, but clearly, we're quibbling over a relatively minor point. Let us get back to the current concern: the interrogation of Lieutenant McCloud by the prosecution. Please proceed, Commander Fields."

"Thank you, Sir. In connection with those weapons, I was about to ask the Lieutenant to reassure us he had no prior knowledge of Markowski's intentions to steal them and use them against the Japanese. Tell us, Lieutenant: Did you?"

"No, Sir, not an inkling. As a matter of fact, when we became aware of the fact he was missing, the thought that he'd gone over on purpose never entered our minds. We assumed he must have fallen overboard and, as a result, we spent the balance of the night searching for him. Then, we had Army Air look for him the day after,

followed by some of our patrolling PT's the next night—
all to no avail, of course."

"I see," said Judge Advocate Fields. "And tell us,
when did you become aware of the fact that Markowski
had not fallen overboard, but had intentionally armed himself and deserted?"

"Objection!" bawled Defense Counsel Trimble.
"There he goes again! The prosecution persists in using
the term 'deserted'! He *must* know better than that by
now! That is what we are here to ascertain. If the court
were to allow it to continue, all the prosecution would
have to prove is that there was a war going on at the time,
and the ball game would be over!"

Captain O'Brien smiled. "'Ball game,' eh? Is that
what we're playing here? But, to make it official, the
objection is sustained. Now, gentlemen, let us agree on
a suitable term. Do you have any objection to 'left
the boat'?"

"Fine," said Trimble.

"Not so fine," countered Fields, "unless we make it
more definitive, like 'left the boat without authorization.'"

Trimble shook his head resignedly. "Well, I suppose
we will have to accept that—as long as it is recognized as
a mere clarification and not the judgment of the court."

"Gentlemen," said Captain O'Brien, "I believe we're
setting a record in nitpicking—justifiable as it might seem
to the defense. To settle it, let us use the term 'left
the boat,' accepting the fact that 'without authorization'
is implied.

"Now, if my recollection is still sound after all of that,
the witness has been asked when he became aware of the
fact that the accused had armed himself and 'left the boat.'
Lieutenant McCloud?"

"Our first clue to it occurred when the coastwatchers came back on the air asking us to pick up Coastwatcher Donegal—and with it, mentioning that they had information regarding Markowski."

"You called that a 'clue,'" said the judge advocate, "meaning you still didn't know what had occurred. Is that correct?"

"Yes, Sir. What's more, we were mystified by the implication that the coastwatchers even *knew* Markowski was missing. You remember, we thought he must have fallen overboard, but all of that occurred *after* Coastwatcher Jollymore had left us."

"I see. And when did you learn the rest of the story?"

"When we returned to pick up Jollymore's predecessor—the Australian named Jerry Donegal."

Maxwell Field nodded. "Thank you, Lieutenant. That will be all for now, but it's conceivable we'll have further questions for you later." Captain O'Brien turned to Trimble. "Your witness, defense counsel."

Lieutenant Commander Trimble rose and approached the witness.

"Lieutenant McCloud, am I correct in believing that you didn't have *any* forewarning that the accused intended to 'leave the boat' at an early opportunity in order to pursue the enemy on his own?"

"That is correct, Sir. None at all."

"But you were aware of the fact that his father had died in the Philippines at the onset of the war?"

"Yes Sir, I was. As a matter of fact, we all were. But to be completely truthful, we didn't know Markowski's whole story until the time of the court of inquiry at Morobe."

"But you knew he had joined the Navy—and the PT boat service in particular—in order to avenge the death of his father?"

"Yes, Sir, we were aware of that."

"Well, then, why were you surprised when he did what he did?"

"First, Sir, we assumed he had achieved his goal: to be part of a crew that was searching for, finding, and engaging the enemy on a regular basis. Second, that any rational person would seek to take on the Japanese army on his own, was a thought so outlandish, it never entered our minds."

"So, can I assume that when you found out what had occurred, you were surprised?"

"Much more than that, Commander. We were amazed—astounded."

Commander Trimble nodded. "I see. Now, another matter. I have been led to believe that subsequently—when you arrested Markowski, and in the period that followed—his conduct has been commendable?"

"Excuse me, Commander, but I believe you are putting nonexisting words in my mouth. I don't think 'commendable' is the right word for it."

"And what word would you suggest we use?"

"Oh, perhaps 'tolerable'—or maybe more accurate would be 'acceptable'—for a person under arrest, that is."

"And further, Lieutenant, I understand that, while being brought to the rear base in Milne Bay, the PT in which he was a prisoner was taken under attack by elements of the Japanese air force. And because the crew was shorthanded, he was asked to participate. It is said that he did so willingly, and that in the resultant foray, his conduct *was* commendable. Do you agree?"

"Well, Sir, since he was riding another boat—and I was not present—anything I might say would merely be hearsay. In that vein, however, I have heard it said that, when asked to participate, he did his assigned job adequately and properly—like the rest of the crew. Again, Sir, I object to the use of the word 'commendable' in the implied sense that what he did was worthy of a commendation."

"Oho, I see we have a legal mind at work here."

McCloud smiled. "Well, thank you, Sir. That *was* my training—until the Japanese interrupted it on December 7th."

The gavel rapped. "Gentlemen, I am sure this aside is fascinating for everyone present, but I suggest we get back to the business at hand. Counselor?"

"Sorry, Sir, I understand," said Trimble. "And now, following up on Lieutenant McCloud's inference that he can't reply on a firsthand basis, as our next witness, I would like to call Lieutenant Paul Corbett—captain of the 143 boat on which Markowski *was* riding."

After the usual swearing in, the defense counselor began anew.

"Lieutenant Corbett, when your boat was taken under attack on the way to the rear base in Milne Bay, you had the accused serve as part of the crew, did you not?"

"Yes, Sir, that is correct—when the attack occurred and for its duration, that is."

"Would you describe it for us?"

"Of course, Sir, but I've covered that matter in writing and have it here."

"That's all very well, Corbett—and we'll enter it as part of the proceedings of this trial. But, redundant as it may be, I suggest you tell it to this court. Would you describe it for us?"

"Of course, Sir. As a result of a recent barge-busting engagement, we had a disabled boat capable of running on only two of its three engines—so even more than usual, a total defense was in order. However, we had two of our men who had been injured in the aforementioned engagement in the crew's quarters, and Markowski and Zachary his guard, in the day room.

"Accordingly, we had Zachary assume his usual station at the after 50 calibers and asked Markowski if he could and would operate the smoke generator if needed."

"And how did he respond?"

"He said yes, he knew how to handle it, and would be willing to do it."

"And what happened after the attack occurred?"

"We took the attacking planes under fire and, running into it, the lead plane swerved, dipping a wing into the sea and crashed. The remaining two were circling for another attack, so we laid smoke and hid out in it."

"That smoke was laid by the accused?"

"If you mean by the smoke generator he was operating, yes!" The gallery tittered.

Judge O'Brien glared. "Lieutenant, that will do! Enough of the levity, gentlemen. Just ask and answer the questions factually and routinely!"

"Sorry, Mr. President—I'm afraid I led us into that. I apologize, Sir." Trimble turned back to Paul Corbett. "And, Lieutenant, in manning that generator, what kind of a job did the accused do?"

"Perfectly competent, Sir."

"Competent? That's all? It wasn't 'commendable'?"

"In that sense. Commander, I must agree with Lieutenant McCloud. He—Markowski—did his job well, properly, willingly, as expected, like the rest of the crew."

The Lieutenant Commander stared at the witness for a long moment, then said, "Thank you, Lieutenant. That will be all."

"Your turn, Judge Advocate," said President O'Brien.

Lieutenant Commander Fields rose, smirked in the direction of his retreating counterpart, then turned to the bench.

"Nothing for this witness at the moment. But if it pleases the court, I would like to proceed with the remainder of our case."

"By all means, Commander, go right ahead."

"As previously stated, for our next witness we were hoping to have James Jollymore, the current coastwatcher in the Lae area, but it was apparent that wouldn't be possible without interrupting the highly important work he is engaged in, even more than we already have—thanks to the defendant over there."

"Objection!" called Trimble. "That aspersion is premature—and unnecessary!"

"Objection sustained," said Judge O'Brien. "Just proceed with your case, Judge Advocate."

"Yes, Sir. I am sorry. For the reason I mentioned, we did the next best thing on the advice of Captain Mooney, Commodore of PT's New Guinea. We had his deposition taken. Unfortunately, in the process the enemy was alerted, gunfire occurred at the beachhead, and Ensign Stringer, executive officer of PT 150 who was carrying the deposition from beach to boat was seriously—and perhaps fatally—injured."

Fields turned and stared at Markowski. "Whether or not that incident can be said to be directly traceable to the actions of the accused may be termed a moot point—but certainly, without the prior action on his part, it would *never* have occurred."

"Objection again!" called his counterpart, Trimble. "That is an intolerable leap from fact to supposition!"

"And objection sustained *again*" ruled President O'Brien. "Strike that from the records—and I urge you members of the court to ignore that innuendo by the prosecution."

Lieutenant Commander Fields nodded. "And sorry *again*, Sir. I understand. But, to get to the point. We have made copies of Mr. Jollymore's deposition and wish to distribute them: one to you, Mr. President, one to each of the members of the court, and here is yours, Defense Counsel. There they are, gentlemen: faithful copies, including a hole from the Japanese bullet that wounded Ensign Stricker."

"Very dramatic!" flared Trimble. "And without the bullet hole, would you have gone to all this trouble?"

"What did I do that wasn't factual and valid?"

The gavel came down—hard. "That will do, gentlemen!"

The judge advocate again smirked at his counterpart, then continued.

"Mr. President, I would like to give each of you time to read the deposition before proceeding further."

President O'Brien nodded. "So ordered." He picked up his copy and perused it. Scanning the court, he then directed, "Proceed, Commander."

Lieutenant Commander Fields began anew. "Mr. President, in addition to the deposition, and in order to give the court an opportunity to further understand exactly what occurred, I would like to call Mr. Jollymore's predecessor, who also witnessed Markowski's behavior ashore after 'leaving the boat': Mr. Jerry Donegal."

President O'Brien leaned over toward the proposed witness.

"Mr. Donegal, you are an Australian citizen, are you not?"

"Aye, Sir—that I am."

"And you realize this is a United States Navy Court, and as such, we have no jurisdiction over you. Nevertheless, as a living, breathing member of the coastwatchers—one who was present when these events occurred—your testimony would be of interest. With that in mind, the court asks your cooperation. Are you willing to give it to us?"

"Aye, Sir. Not only am I willing to do so, but my direct superior, Commander Eric Feldt, has asked me to be as helpful as possible."

"Fine. The court understands and appreciates it. Commander Fields, as judge advocate, would you please read the oath to Mr. Donegal? And, Mr. Donegal, this is the same oath we are using for members of our Navy. I hope you can go along with it."

"Aye, Sir, I'll do my best." The oath was read and accepted routinely.

Lieutenant Commander Fields began his interrogation of the Australian.

"Let me add my appreciation of your cooperation, Mr. Donegal. Now, will you tell us about yourself—in particular, your experience and background that led Commander Feldt to choose you for the job at Lae?"

"Well, Sir, for a number of years I worked at various jobs at ANGAU—"

"That's the Australia-New Guinea Administration Unit?"

"Yes, that's fair dink—aah, that is correct. And five of those years were in the port director's office at Lae—until the Nips moved in, that is."

"Which made you a logical choice for the job?"

"S'treuth as far as movements in and out of the port and its airfield were concerned."

"You seem to be qualifying that. Did you have any deficiencies?"

"Aye—you see, I wasn't well acquainted in the never-never."

Maxwell Fields frowned. "The 'never-never'?"

"Aye—the back country—and with the bushies."

"By 'back country,' you mean the area surrounding Lae—the countryside?"

"Aye, and it's a toughie. A good place to hide and still be able to watch and report on what the Nips at Lae are up to."

"I understand. And by 'bushies' you mean...?"

"The natives living in the nev—the outlying area."

"And tell us, Mr. Donegal, how long were you alone in that—that outlying area?"

"Oh, a tad over a year."

"My, that's a long time. I gather you asked to be relieved of your duties?"

"No, I didn't. That was Jollymore's idea, when he came to fix the squawker—the radio."

"You didn't like that decision of his?"

"No, the good oil is I was glad he did. I'd had enough."

"All right," said Fields, "we understand and appreciate all that background information. Now, to get to the case at hand. While you were at your highly secret sanctuary, you did see the accused, Markowski?"

"Hell's bells, aye! I was just there for a short time after Jollymore arrived, but he—Markowski over there—showed up nearly every day."

"And what had he been doing?"

"It seems a lame-brainer—hard to understand—but he'd been out looking for Japs to kill. Had his own little old war underway."

"But why did he keep showing up at your hideaway?"

"He wanted to rest, jabber—and have some nosh."

"'Nosh'?"

"Aye, some din-din—*food*."

"And you didn't like that?

"By Cripes—no!" First, our rations are limited. Second, we're supposed to be quiet as lame mice: just watch and report on the Nips. The last thing we wanted was to have some bludger rort the system—"

Commander Fields held up a hand. "Hold on Mr. Donegal—what's a 'bludger'?"

"Why, that's an imbo who lives off of someone else."

"And an 'imbo'?"

"That's an imbecile. Excuse me, perhaps I shouldn't have said that. But, s'treuth is he made us mad as cut snakes."

Judge Advocate Fields smiled tolerantly. "Let's go back a bit—it seems we're just getting in deeper as far as mutual comprehension is concerned. You said he might 'rort the system.' I want to be sure everyone understands completely. What would that be in simple English?"

"Why, change the rules. As we kept telling him, we only wanted to be left alone—but he wouldn't do it. We didn't want the Nips tailing him up to us and...ah...queering our whole deal."

"So, when your radio was back on the air, you asked the Americans to get the accused out of your hair?"

"Aye," smiled the bald Australian rubbing his head, "if you want to put it that way, that's the full two-bob."

"Thank you, Mr. Donegal." Fields turned to Captain O'Brien. "I believe, Sir, this testimony parallels what you'll find in Mr. Jollymore's deposition. And, with that, I've finished with this witness."

"All right, Commander Fields. Now, Commander Trimble, as counsel for the defense, it's your turn."

"No questions, Mr. President."

"No cross examination!"

"No, Sir. With what we've just heard, plus Mr. Jollymore's deposition, the facts have been brought out nicely."

The president studied the defense counsel intently— then shook his head.

"You're sure?"

Commander Trimble nodded complacently. "Yes, Sir—I'm sure."

The gavel came down. "In that case we'll break for lunch."

17

Commander Trimble and Markowski had their lunch aboard the *Bay City*, choosing a corner table for its relative privacy—the best one could hope to find in the crowded and noisy mess hall. Midway through the meal, Commander Trimble broke the silence.

"How is it going, Markowski?"

"Oh fine, Sir. This is the best meal I've had in a long time."

His counsel smiled. "That's very nice. But, what I was referring to was the trial. What's your impression thus far?"

Markowski's brow wrinkled. "I...I'm not sure, Sir."

"And why not?"

"Well, all I've heard is them telling their side of the story."

"Their side of the story? All I've heard them bring out are the facts. How can we dispute them? Was there something wrong with them that I missed?"

"No, not really, Sir. But the way it was told, it made me look like the bad guy."

"Made you look like the bad guy? Don't you get it, Markowski? You did it to yourself! You *are* the bad guy!"

"But...but, Sir, we never asked the witnesses—the coastwatcher and Lieutenant McCloud—any questions."

"Any questions? What would you have me ask? Did they say anything that wasn't true?"

"No...no, I guess they didn't—but what they said, and the way they said it, made me look real bad."

"Markowski! Don't you get it? You are charged with 'desertion in time of war.' It's a clear-cut case. Can you dispute that?"

"No, I guess I can't. But don't you think my case is different? I had reasons for doing what I did. Aren't we going to tell that? Tell my side of the story?"

"Of course we are—at the proper time. But, we're a long way from that point. They're simply in the process of telling what you did, showing that you're guilty of the charge. That's their job, and they're doing it quite well."

"Guilty! You mean we're going to change and say I'm guilty?"

"No, no—only on the minor charge of theft, that is. You must have heard me say—or infer—we are pleading 'not guilty' several times, didn't you?"

"Yes, Sir, but that's the only thing I've heard. When are we going to do something about...about showing I'm innocent?"

Commander Trimble slammed the table with both hands loud enough to cause others to look around, including Judge Advocate Fields across the room, who smiled knowingly.

Commander Trimble waggled a finger in his charge's face.

"As I've been *trying* to tell you, it's impossible to state you're innocent and it's high time you get used to it. Every witness—everybody on that stand, including you—will be used to show you're guilty. Young man, you must understand proving otherwise is impossible. You're guilty as sin!"

"But, Commander, Sir, you had me plead 'not guilty'...and now you say I'm 'guilty.' Why...why has that changed?"

"It hasn't. Sure you're guilty, but, hopefully, not of desertion. That's the key word, my boy: 'Desertion.' If they succeed in hanging that on you—'Desertion,' *period*—that ball game of yours is over!"

"I think I see what you mean. But, didn't you say we were going to tell my side of the story: *Why* I did it?"

"Now you're getting it. We are, young man—in due time. This is merely the prosecution's turn at bat. We'll be next."

— —

President O'Brien rapped the gavel persistently.

"Order—the court will come to order!"

This time, however, it wasn't easy. There was more of it to come to order, more onlookers, as word of the unusual nature of the trial continued to spread throughout the base. Finally, the court did quiet down to O'Brien's satisfaction. He turned to the judge advocate.

"Commander Fields, please continue."

Judge Advocate Fields rose and took the few steps necessary to face the court—the larger court of onlookers as well as members of the court itself.

"Gentlemen: The accused is charged with 'Desertion in Time of War.'" He smiled waggishly. "I believe no one—the defense included—will contest our belief that we are engaged in a war." He looked at his counterpart. "Can we consider that portion of the charge a 'fait accompli'?" Commander Trimble merely shrugged.

"If that means you acquiesce, I thank you," said Fields. "That leaves us with only three questions to be answered. One: Did the accused desert his post? Two: Did he carry out an unauthorized war with the enemy? And three: Did he steal government equipment issued to PT 150 and put it to his own use?

"As to number one: We heard Lieutenant McCloud, skipper of the 150 boat, testify to the accused's desertion—excuse me, his 'leaving his post and the boat' with no challenge from the defense—and the same regarding theft of equipment issued to the PT."

"Not quite," interrupted Trimble. "I object to that so-called summary of our position, Mr. President. Although it is true we pleaded 'guilty' to the charge of theft, the prior acquisition of the gun and its ammunition in question is of dubious legality itself. The government equipment in question was not issued to the boat. It was an illicit gift, if not a bribe, to Lieutenant McCloud from a Marine officer in order to gain a ride on his PT boat."

"Perhaps not issued to the boat per se," interjected the judge advocate, "but undeniably government issue."

"All right, gentlemen," groaned President O'Brien, "let us accept the point as clarified. Proceed, Commander Fields."

"In order to emphasize the seriousness of the offense, we provided the testimony of one of the coastwatchers, and the deposition of the other, attesting to the potential

153

threat to their vital contribution to the war effort—to say nothing of their very lives.

"Additionally, gentlemen, the prosecution would like to point out the additional exposure this willful and unlawful action of the accused caused to our PT's themselves. Unfortunately, it is meaningfully—and hopefully not tragically—demonstrated in the serious wounding of Ensign Stringer, executive officer of PT 150."

Commander Fields looked up at the presiding officer, then turned to the rest of the court. Palms upturned, he spread his hands.

"Gentlemen, what else needs to be proved? If ever I saw an open-and-shut case, this is it. And with that, the prosecution rests."

Captain O'Brien turned to the defense counsel. "I must admit this is a weird one, and at this point I am inclined to agree with that truncated, and perhaps premature, summation of the judge advocate: 'What else needs to be proved?' Since no cross-examination has yet been made, does that mean the defense has no defense?"

Lieutenant Commander Trimble smiled in response. "Mr. President, the defense can readily understand the court's bewilderment at this point. The accused has been charged with 'desertion in time of war,' and we must admit the judge advocate has done a commendable job of delineating and summing up the case for the prosecution."

The president stared down at the defense counsel quizzically. "Excuse me, Commander Trimble, but your apparent submissiveness continues to mystify me. I have been under the impression that the accused is pleading 'not guilty' to the major charge. Does this mean you are altering that?"

"Oh no, Sir—far from it. I can understand that it must seem confusing—confusing at this point, that is. As the prosecution has stated, on the surface this seems a simple case—but, as we fully intend to show, it is far, far from that. The court will see that explored before a full, fair, and well-defined picture of the matter can be considered."

"Objection," came the call from Judge Advocate Fields. "The prosecution believes it has proved its case and, further, even the defense is admitting the guilt of the accused. He's moving on to mitigating circumstances."

Trimble laughed. "Hardly, Commander Fields—that will come later. But, as of now, are you saying that no questions should remain in the court's mind, such as *why* the accused did what he did? Come now!"

The gavel came down. "Enough of this wrangling. Spectators: Please leave the room temporarily." The spectators filed out grumpily, only to be called back in after a few minutes.

President O'Brien announced, "The objection is overruled—unanimously. The defense counsel's supposition has proved correct: Curiosity has won the day. Before it deliberates as to the guilt of the accused, the court would like to know *why* the accused acted as he did. Please enlighten us, Commander Trimble."

"In that event," smiled Trimble, "and to get at the answer authoritatively, we would like to call on our prime witness, the accused himself—Motor Machinist's Mate Third Class Myron Markowski."

Markowski took the stand and the oath. His pallor was striking, his nervousness manifest in a licking of lips and strained clenching of hands while scrutinizing the courtroom from his new perspective.

155

"Calm down, boy," murmured Commander Trimble, "we'll take it slow and easy." With that, Trimble turned to the court. "We ask your indulgence: this young man, inexperienced in the environment and procedures of a courtroom—"

"Objection!" growled Fields. "The accused is mature enough to have wormed his way into the Navy—legally or illegally, and—"

Crack! came the gavel. "Stop it—both of you! Now, please proceed, Counselor—and the unembellished facts will serve very nicely."

Trimble nodded. "I understand, Mr. President. As I was saying, we ask your indulgence. The accused has been through a great deal, before, during, and after the action in question. Throughout the entire series of events, he has been eager to tell the *full* side of his story and its rationale. But up to this point it has not been related entirely—much less examined in sufficient depth. That, as you will see, is regrettable, for he does have a tale of high interest—loaded with justification for his actions."

"Objection!" came the expected call. "Again! Let the accused tell his story, yes—but certainly it is up to the court, not the defense counsel, to adjudge its degree of pertinence and justification for his subsequent acts."

"Objection sustained," ruled Captain O'Brien. "The prosecution is correct. Just give us the facts, Counselor. We'll form our own opinions."

"Sorry, Mr. President," smiled Trimble. "You are right, of course. We're perfectly content with that." He turned back to his charge. "Now, Markowski, you admit you left your station at a time when you knew full well we were at war, didn't you?"

"Y...yes, Sir."

"All right, then; the time has come. We want you to tell us *why* you did it—the whole story, please."

As one man, members of the court and onlookers alike leaned forward, their curiosity overwhelmingly palpable.

Markowski swallowed with difficulty. "Because... because of what they did to my father, Sir."

"Your father? Tell us, who is your father?"

"It isn't *is*. Sir—it's *was*. He's dead. But...but he was Master Sergeant Matthew Markowski of the United States Marines."

"He was a career Marine?"

"Yes, Sir, all his life—that *was* his life."

"Was he a good one?"

"Objection!" blurted Judge Advocate Fields. "That's asking for a personal opinion. What in the world would you expect a son to say?"

"Sustained," said the president. "Please, just stick to the facts, Counselor."

Trimble acquiesced. "I understand your directions perfectly. Sir, but if it pleases the court, the fact of Markowski's close and admiring relationship with and for his father has a *great* deal to do with his subsequent actions. We ask your indulgence."

"We'll see, Commander Trimble. Now, proceed—more cautiously, however."

The defense counsel turned back to his client.

"Let me phrase it differently. Markowski, tell the court: What did *you* think of your father?"

"Objection!" came the call. "It's the same thing!"

"Oh no, it isn't," countered Trimble. "I didn't ask him what the rest of the world thought of his father—only what *he* did. Again, his answer is *absolutely fundamental* to this trial!"

"Clear the courtroom!"

The reconvention of the court and spectators occurred in a surprisingly short time.

After a repeated rapping of the gavel, and the resultant quiet, O'Brien spoke.

"Although, to some extent, we are inclined to agree with the judge advocate that the defense seems to be splitting hairs, the objection is overruled—at least, it is until we can ascertain just what the defense is getting at. Proceed, Counselor."

"Thank you, Sir. Now, go ahead Markowski, and tell us what *you* thought of your father—as a Marine, that is."

"Oh, the Marine Corps, that was his whole life. He was tremendously proud of the corps, his country, and his part in it. And I, Sir, am—or was—proud of him."

"Objection! For the same reason!" came the predictable call. "Sir, this is getting maudlin in the extreme. It's merely a son's naturally prejudiced opinion—it's not the least bit factual—or pertinent!"

"Oh, yes it is," bristled Trimble. "And with the exercise of a little of the patience the president has requested, you will see it has *everything* to do with the course of events—and the trial."

"And, again, overruled." President O'Brien pointed at the judge advocate. "Commander Fields, the court joins the defense in reemphasizing its request for your forbearance. Let us hear him out, *then* make our judgment."

A red-faced Fields flared, "The next thing he'll be telling us is that he loves his mother!"

The gavel came down hard—so much so that the president raised the handle to the light to see if he had broken it. Satisfied, he pointed it at the irate lieutenant commander.

"*Again*—and, hopefully, for the last time on this issue, Mr. Judge Advocate, you are out of order! You are trying the patience of this court most severely!"

In turn, President O'Brien turned to the defense counsel.

"On the other hand, to be fair, I must admit this is an unusual case, and at this point, can understand and, to a degree, sympathize with the judge advocate's succinct summation: 'What else needs to be proved—or disproved?' Defense Counselor, can we get to the point?"

Commander Trimble nodded. "Mr. President, the defense can readily understand the court's current bewilderment. The specification charges the accused with 'desertion in time of war,' and from what has been presented thus far, we agree that it *seems* to have been proven."

The president peered down at the defense counsel curiously.

"Excuse me, Commander Trimble, but I am confused. I must ask again: Does this mean the accused is now pleading guilty?"

A rueful-appearing defense counselor replied, "If it pleases the court, the answer to that has to be 'yes—but no.'"

"Now I *am* perplexed," said Captain O'Brien. "This case seems to be going around in circles. Counselor, you'll have to clarify that statement."

"As I said previously, I don't blame the court for being perplexed—at this point, that is. However, to aid in straightening out those circles, we readily concede that, at first glance, this seems a simple case and the accused should plead guilty. But—and this is the point—he is *never* going to plead guilty to a charge of desertion. 'Left the boat' —yes; but 'deserted' —no. And to elucidate the difference, I would like to proceed with the testimony of the accused."

"By all means," said O'Brien, "go right ahead."

"Now, Markowski," said Trimble, turning back to the accused, "we were talking about your father. You told us he was a career Marine—and in your opinion, a good one. Is that correct?"

"It certainly is, Sir."

"What kind of life did you have with him?"

"Oh, we moved around a lot, all over the country, and when he was overseas, we just waited for him to return."

"So, I assume you went to various schools?"

"Yes, Sir—quite a few."

"Didn't that bother you?"

"At times—but, mostly, I found it interesting."

"Interesting? How about your mother—did she find it 'interesting' too?"

"No, she kept saying she was looking forward to the time when we could settle down in one place."

"All right, Markowski. Now let's get to the point of this case."

"And that would be salutary," interjected Commander Fields. "It's about time!"

As expected, the gavel cracked. "Enough of that, Judge Advocate. Proceed, Counselor Trimble."

"Where were you living when the war broke out— ours with Japan?"

"In San Diego, waiting for my father to come home."

"Waiting for him to come home? Did he?"

"No, Sir. You see, he was stationed in the Philippines— in a place called Bataan."

"Oh my—that wasn't a good place to be at that time, was it?"

"No, Sir, it sure wasn't. He fought in the war and ended up in the thing they called 'The Death March.'"

"The Death March! And what happened to him?"

"It was terrible, Sir. He was beaten, tortured—badly tortured by those Japanese...then they killed him."

"Really? Now, in general, we are well aware of that Death March in all its pain and agony, but since the Philippines are still in the hands of the enemy, the specifics are unusually hard to come by. How do you know your father was 'beaten, tortured, and killed by the Japanese?'"

"We—my mother, that is—received a letter from a survivor of the Death March, a Marine corporal who had served with my father."

Trimble continued the rehearsed probe. "A letter from a survivor of the Death March? They're a rare breed. And aren't those who did survive in Japanese prison camps?"

"Yes, Sir. I understand that's true in most cases—but this one is different. You see. Sir, this particular Marine corporal was on a Japanese prison ship on its way to Japan and it was torpedoed and sunk by one of our own submarines. As one of the few survivors, he was picked up by the sub."

"And then what did he do?"

"He must have had a lot of time to think about it and write before he got home, because his letter is kind of long. It..." Markowski choked, then inhaled deeply before continuing, "Sorry, Sir, but it hurts to think about what it says."

Trimble walked over and put a hand on Markowski's shoulder. "Take it easy, son. Now, tell us: *Is this the letter?*"

Markowski took the letter, paged through it briefly, then said, "Yes, Sir—that's a copy of it."

"Objection!" called Fields. "There is something wrong here. This is the first time the prosecution has even been aware of the existence of this piece of evidence."

Trimble retorted, "Let me remind the prosecution that, by its own hypothesis, the trial, per se, is over. It infers it has proved its case, and the accused is guilty, to which we say they may be partially right. Guilty, perhaps, but, if it pleases the court, we reiterate: *not guilty of desertion.*"

Lieutenant Commander Fields rejoined the argument: "The counselor is leaping to conclusions—conclusions that are the prerogative of the court. All we said—based on what the defense had presented up to that point—was 'what is there left to prove?' Now, in response, the defense is offering new evidence—evidence not heretofor revealed."

"Mr. President," said Trimble, "I can well understand the prosecution's complaint. Although we have known of the existence of this letter for some time, we have only recently received a copy of the letter itself." Trimble walked over to his table and picked up some papers. "Here you are, gentlemen: a copy for the court, and one for the prosecution."

Judge Advocate Fields leafed through the letter, then looked quizzically at his counterpart. "This is merely an unauthenticated letter. Where is the deposition?"

Trimble smiled wearily. "I don't blame you, Judge Advocate. We, too, have been pursuing it to that end—

futilely, I might add. And that's the main reason you haven't seen it before. You see, we have found a deposition more than a bit difficult to produce since the author, Marine Corporal Herbert Reynolds, is currently, importantly, unavailably occupied in the fracas somewhere over on the island of Bougainville. All we have are the assurances of Mrs. Matthew Markowski that the letter is genuine."

He turned to the court. "Gentlemen, in clarifying the issue, we only wish to explain *why* the accused did what he did. We could do so without the letter—and will if necessary. But since the letter was an important factor in the thinking of the accused, we are merely doing our best to take you down the route that led him to the actions in question today. Further, we believe this letter adds authority and realism to what would otherwise be the solely personal testimony of the accused.

"In other words, gentlemen, the experiences reiterated in this letter were the basis for a goodly portion of the defendant's raison d'etre. Surely, the court wants to be privy to that!"

The gavel banged. "Clear the court!"

When the court reconvened, President O'Brien affirmed, "The court agrees with the defense: The letter should serve as a step in the reasoning that led the accused to do what he did—nothing more. On that basis, please continue, Counselor."

"Thank you, Sir. I will read the letter, but before doing so, I wish to reiterate the testimony of the accused to the fact that he is a great admirer of the man his father was. That is correct, isn't it, Markowski?"

"Good Lord!" raged Commander Fields. "Must we go through that again?"

The gavel tapped. "Remember our request for patience while we hear out the counselor. Please proceed, Commander Trimble."

"Thank you, Captain. Now, Markowski, to repeat: Isn't it true you admired your father greatly?"

"Yes, Sir. You see, since he was a career Marine, our entire life was built around the corps and his part in it. I never knew any other life."

"We understand. Now, tell us more about this father you admired so much. What did he look like? And just how did you feel about him?"

"My dad was a large, rugged-looking man. We always said he could have been the man on the Marine recruiting poster. And, as to my feelings about him, Sir, I guess you could say I worshipped him. He was—was and is—not just my father, but my hero. I only wish I could be just like him."

The defense counselor turned to the court. "Now, gentlemen, keep that in mind while I read this letter—a letter written objectively—not by any member of the Markowski family, but *to* them by an outsider. And, while I do so, imagine if you can, the feelings of this lad as he read it—or heard it read for the first time."

"Objection!" came the call from Judge Advocate Fields. "Again, these theatrics are unnecessary. They're sentimental and maudlin, an obvious attempt to sway and soften the objective reasoning of this court."

President O'Brien glared at Fields. "Judge Advocate, *you* are the one who is overdoing it. The court finds Commander Trimble's proposed rendition appropriate, and your description of it, conversely inappropriate."

"Sorry, Sir. I accept the rebuke."

"All right, Commander Fields. Now, proceed Commander Trimble."

Trimble smiled wryly at Fields, then returned to the court.

"Thank you, Mr. President. Here, then, is the letter from a Marine colleague, about Master Sergeant Matthew Markowski."

Dear Mrs. Markowski,

This is not an easy letter for me to write, and I realize it is going to be even worse for you to read. But, knowing how difficult it is to get information out of the Philippines at this time, I feel honor-bound to write to the family of the man I knew so well and admired so much.

Matt and I were fellow Marines on Bataan— and after position-after-position was overrun and taken by the Japanese, we—Matt and I—became part of its final resistance.

With the others, we hoped for, and expected, Uncle Sam to come to our aid, but when that didn't occur—well, here are our sentiments, as expressed by some wag who spoke for us all:

We're the battling bastards of Bataan,
No mama, no papa, no Uncle Sam,
No aunts, no uncles, no nephews, no nieces,
No rifles, no planes or artillery pieces—
And nobody gives a damn.

At any rate, Mrs. Markowski, since it became obvious that our days—or hours—on the peninsula were numbered, I joined Matt in finding and persuading a native boatman to sneak us over to Corregidor at night.

As you probably know, Bataan did fall to the Japanese, and The Rock, being the last remaining bastion of United States defense activity, became their next target.

Matt and I helped man the few operational batteries left on Corregidor and, in the final assault, the smaller weapons.

Finally, however, on May 6th, General Wainwright surrendered and the Nips took us back to Bataan to join the stragglers of that miserable ordeal—the one they are now calling "The Death March"—to the Jap prison camp at Cabanatuan.

That march took 12 days, but it seemed like 112. Most of us were sick to begin with: malaria, dysentery, beri-beri, lack of food—you name it, we had it. The Japs were gleeful—had a ball making life—and death—miserable for all of us. Everyone suffered terribly, but some more than others.

That brave husband of yours seemed to get special attention—probably because he seemed in pretty good shape and looked like an American master sergeant should look. After a few days, they—the Nips—were picking on a private we knew—hooting and laughing as they beat him with their rifles. Finally, Matt couldn't stand it any more and he tried to help the poor guy—and that gave the Nips their excuse to turn on *him*.

I don't know how to say this in a kind way, Mrs. M. They killed him. I won't go in to the details, except to say they took their time doing it. But he—Matt—died like the great man he was—which seemed to make the Nips all the madder. I guess they thought only a Japanese could do that. All I can say to all of you is that you can be awfully proud of him. As his friend, I know I am.

When this damned war is over, I'll tell you where I am. Then, when you need a favor or two, I want you to call on me. I want to do that. I owe the Markowski family a million of them.

God bless you all,

Herb Reynolds, Corporal USMC

"There." Commander Trimble replaced the letter on his desk. "That's it—a difficult letter for all." He looked over at his counterpart at the prosecution desk. "And I trust that it wasn't too hard on you. Commander."

For the first time, Fields looked contrite. "Just trying to my job, Trimble."

President O'Brien rapped his gavel. "Enough of that, you two. Don't get personal."

"Sorry, Sir," said Trimble, "and you too, Commander. But, speaking of getting personal, I'd like to get back to the personal interrogation of the accused."

"Proceed, Counselor."

Trimble turned back to Markowski. "After receiving the letter we've just heard, what was your reaction?"

Markowski bowed his head, murmuring something.

His counselor commanded, "Speak up, Markowski. I know this isn't easy—and hasn't been since that letter arrived. But I'm sure the court wants to hear what you have to say."

The accused straightened up in his chair. "Sorry, Sir, and you're right. It isn't easy. It hasn't been since I first read that letter. But, I knew then what I wanted to do...I knew I wanted to get them."

"Get them? Get who?"

"The Japs, Sir—as many as I could."

"And what did you do about it?"

"Well, Sir, first I went to the local Marine recruiting office and tried to enlist, but they turned me down."

"Because of age? The truth now, Markowski."

"Yes, partly that. I was seventeen, but I told the recruiting fellow I was eighteen."

"But he found out differently, and that's why he turned you down?"

"That was part of it, Sir."

"Part of it? What is the other part?"

"Well, Sir, first he sent me to a doctor for an examination—and, after it, the doctor told the recruiting sergeant I was unfit—'*psychologically* unfit,' he said."

"What did he mean by that?"

"I'm really not sure, Sir. All I know is that he and I didn't get along very well. I didn't expect their doctor to be like that. He wasn't at all like my dad."

"What do you mean by that? Tell us about it."

"You're sure you want me to?"

"Yes, I'm sure. Go ahead."

"Well, this fellow—the doctor—asked me all kinds of goofy questions, things that didn't have anything to do with being a Marine and fighting Japs."

"Goofy questions? Like what?"

"Like, 'Do you like girls?' And...and...'how often do you masterbate'?"

"Really? And what did you tell him?"

"I said, 'Sure I like girls.' But about that other thing, I told him I didn't think it was any of his goldarned business. Besides that, he found out I was really only seventeen, and that's when he told the sergeant I was a 'psychologically unfit kid.'"

"What did the recruiting sergeant do about it?"

"Well, he laughed about the 'psychologically unfit' story, but since I was only seventeen, he said I'd have to get my mother's permission to sign up, and she...she wouldn't give it to me."

"She wouldn't? Why not?"

"She said she'd already lost a husband in the war, and didn't want to lose a son, too."

"So what did you do next?"

"Well, Sir, I'd heard about Bulkeley and the other PT boat fellows—the ones who got General MacArthur out of the Philippines. That sounded like it might be the next best thing for me, so I went back to the courthouse and down the hall to the Navy recruiting office and spoke to the chief petty officer in charge. I told him I'd sign up for the Navy if he would get me into PT boats. He seemed like a nice guy and he said that if I passed the physical and signed up, he'd do his best."

"'He'd do his best' Mmmm—and with that, you signed up?"

"Sure. As I said, I liked the fellow—and his doctor too. He wasn't at all like the other one. He didn't ask me any of those nutty questions. So I signed up."

"But how did you get your mother's permission this time?"

"I didn't need it—the chief never found out I was only seventeen."

"You lied and got away with it this time?"

"Yes, Sir, that's right. I guess I've always looked kind of old for my age."

"But, how about your mother. Didn't she object?"

"No," smiled Markowski, "I didn't tell her about the PT boat part. I just said I'd probably be floating around on a nice, big, safe battleship."

"I see. *Then* what occurred?"

Oh, that recruiting chief turned out to be a man of his word. I went to boot camp at Great Lakes, and following that to MTBSTC."

"You had better spell that out for us."

"That means 'Motor Torpedo Boats Squadrons Training Center.' It's at Melville, Rhode Island, on Narragansett Bay."

"So you got what you wanted?"

"Well, Sir, in a way—and in another way, I didn't."

"You'd better explain that to the court."

"Oh, I got into 'The Boats" all right—and got along just fine at the Training Center. But in the end, they made me an engineer."

"They made you an engineer? What was wrong with that? As I understand it, you were sent to an outbound squadron, you ended up in New Guinea, and you did fight the Japanese. Isn't that everything you wanted?"

"Again, Sir, my answer has to be 'yes—but no.' Yes, we did get to fight the Japs, but no, *I* didn't. You see, Sir, I was stuck down in the engine room helping to nurse those big Packard engines—and, no matter what was happening above, *I never saw any of it!*"

"And you didn't like that?"

"No, Sir, I sure didn't. You see, Sir, I wanted to get revenge for what they did to my dad—real, personal revenge, not just to hear what a swell time the guys topside were having doing it."

"And that is why you took the skipper's carbine, ammunition for it, a machete, and some food, then slipped off the boat in enemy-held waters?"

"Yes, Sir, that's...that's right."

"And tell us, Markowski, what was you plan? What did you want to do?"

"I...I wanted to get me some Japs—like I said, because of what they did to my dad."

"And why did you follow the coastwatcher—the one with the happy name?"

"Oh, Mr. Jollymore! I heard he could see Japs from his place, so I figured if I followed him, I could find me some Japs—and know where to get some help if I needed it."

"Now, Markowski, tell us. Did it work out that way?"

"Well, Sir, yes I found out where the Japs were all right. But when I went back to where Mr. Jollymore and Mr. Donegal were, they didn't seem very pleased to see me."

"So we understand. But did it work out all right for you? Did you kill some Japs?"

"Yes, a few—but it was harder than I thought it would be."

171

"Harder? In what way?"

"Well, first that's awfully rough country and I wasn't as well equipped as I wish I had been. And, also, it wasn't easy to find one or two all by themselves. And, besides that, they weren't any patsies, Sir. They're tough!"

"I see. Now, Markowski, let's go back a bit. You've admitted that you took some government property and 'slipped off the boat.' But, according to your testimony, I gather that *if* you had been in another position on the 150 boat—say in a topside battle station—you would not have 'left the boat.'"

Judge Advocate Fields came to his feet. "Objection! The counsel is engaging in an intolerable leading of the witness. It's bad enough that the counselor is putting suppositions in the mind of the accused, but now he's putting the answers to those suppositions in his mouth as well! We're supposed to be getting the response of the witness, not that of the defense counselor!"

"Objection sustained," agreed President O'Brien. "You know better than that, Defense Counselor. We know what you are getting at, but as Commander Fields suggests, we want you to phrase it in a way to ellicit your client's response, not yours."

"Sorry, Sir, and I understand the objection." Trimble turned back to his client and winked surreptitiously. "Markowski, if you had been in a topside battle station, would that have satisfied you?"

"Yes, Sir, I believe it would have."

"And, in that case, would you have 'slipped over the side' and followed Mr. Jollymore in order to find the Japanese to hunt?"

"No, Sir, I don't think I would have."

The defense counselor nodded, then turned to the court. "Gentlemen, that completes my interrogation for the time being. However, I would like to reserve the right to go further later on"—and he glanced at the judge advocate—"if it should prove necessary."

"Granted," said President O'Brien. Then, pointing at Commander Fields, he said, "And would the judge advocate like to interrogate the accused at this juncture?"

"Yes, Sir. I certainly would."

"I understand, but it's been a long day and I believe we'll all benefit from an adjournment until tomorrow. We'll begin with your interrogation of the accused at 0900 in the morning, Judge Advocate."

He hit the desk with the gavel. "The court stands adjourned."

18

The court and its onlookers dispersed rapidly, with Markowski and his counselor repairing to the *Bay City* and its small office near the brig while enjoying welcome glasses of cold soft drinks.

Commander Trimble raised his glass in a salute; Markowski followed suit and their glasses clinked.

The counselor grinned. "Here's to a good day. I thought it went quite well. How about you? Do you feel any better about it now?"

Markowski nodded. "Yes, Sir, I *guess* I do. At least, it felt good to be able to tell *why* I did it. But, Sir, I must admit I'm still not happy about one thing."

"Oh, and what is that?"

"Well, Sir, the trial is almost over, isn't it?"

"Not quite, but, yes, we're getting closer. What's your problem?"

"I guess maybe you've heard this before, but even though I've pleaded not guilty, everything that happens seems to say that isn't true—that I *am* guilty. What good is all this explaining now?"

"Plenty, we hope. You're right on one count: As I've told you before, we had no option but to admit your guilt—in part, my boy, just in part. We would have looked like horses' rear ends if we hadn't. After all, there *is* a war going on. You *did* take gun, ammunition, machete, and food, and you *did* leave your post to take on the whole Nip army yourself."

"Yes, but—"

"Wait, young man, let me finish. You must recall that your plea is 'not guilty' on the desertion charge—but that doesn't mean you're innocent. Far from it. You are guilty of leaving your post, the theft, and the unauthorized war. Make no mistake; you are going to be punished for it."

"Well then—"

"Hold on, Markowski. There is nothing in Naval Law that says leaving your assigned post is okay just because you think you have a good personal reason for doing it—not one damned thing!"

An ashen-faced Markowski stammered, "Well, Sir, if...if that is true..."

"It is, son, believe me."

"Then...then why are we going through all this...all this..."

"Interrogation?"

"Yes, Sir. Isn't it just a big waste of time?"

"No, of course it isn't. You must remember that if the prosecution proves its case, you are guilty of 'desertion in time of war,' and like it or not, you also must recall the punishment for that can be severe in the extreme—even death."

"Oh my God! I thought that was over! You don't think..."

"All I can say is that I sincerely hope and believe it won't come to that—and I will do everything I can to obviate it. But, you must have noted we are basing our hopes on the fact that, although you did leave the boat without authorization in time of war, we are claiming that you are not guilty of desertion—and that distinction is the tough part to sell.

"Additionally, after the verdict—and assuming you are adjudged guilty, we will be speaking in mitigation—"

"Miti...mitigation. Tell me again, Sir, what is that?"

"Mitigation consists of stating the reasons why the sentence you receive should be less severe than it would normally be. It means moderation, a reduction in severity. Understand?"

"No, Sir—not really. If the sentence has already been given, wh...what good does it do to ask the court to change it afterwards? Isn't that just a waste of time?"

"Oh, I see why you're confused—and I can't blame you. Here is the sequence of events: First, we will complete this trial—that is, both sides have had their say; all facts have been given in evidence; the court has deliberated and made their decision—guilty or not guilty—and, if its 'guilty,' recommended a penalty. Then, and only then, I will speak in mitigation, knowing that, following the trial the whole matter will go to the Convening Authority for review. *Then*—and not until then—the entire act is over and the final curtain comes down."

Markowski looked baffled. "The Convening Authority? Who is that?"

"Why, as I thought I had explained before, the head of the Seventh Fleet: Admiral Woodstock."

Markowski's bafflement turned to wonder: "The *Admiral* is going to review my case?"

Trimble broke out in laughter: "In a way, yes—but I doubt if he'll do it personally. He has a war to run, you know. When we speak of 'the admiral'—COMNAVSOWESPAC—"

"Wow! That's harder than 'Markowski'!"

Trimble grinned. "No, no, that's not his name—it's his title. It means 'Commander of the Navy, Southwest Pacific'. And when I said he'd review it, I meant his staff would."

"And, Sir, who is that?"

"Oh, his is a big job, as you can imagine. Accordingly, he has a sizeable organization to assist him.Included in it is a legal group—including fellows like Commander Fields and me. He and his legal staff will be your final jury except—and here you'd better hold on tight, my boy—except for the President."

Markowski's jaw *really* dropped open. "The *President!* of the *United States?*"

"Yes, he's the one. But, remember that would only be in the case of a death sentence. Otherwise—and we hope, most likely—this court and that legal staff of the Admiral's are our real and final targets...got it?"

"Yes, Sir, I see. And what happens next—here in the court?"

"We convene at 0900 tomorrow—and that's when your dear friend. Commander Fields, is going to have his turn at you...and, believe me, son, it isn't going to be easy for you!"

"But why? Why is he mad at me?"

Trimble smiled. "He isn't mad at you. But he has a job to do—and as you are seeing, he's good at it. He'll do his level best to get you riled up. But, hear me, my boy: *Don't* you let him do it! And remember, whenever necessary, I'll be backing you up."

"Oh, I know that. Commander. And, Sir—don't think I don't appreciate it."

His defense counsel grinned. "You don't have to thank me."

"I don't?"

"No, you don't. In a way, I'm like your pal, Judge Advocate Fields—I've got a job to do."

19

The following day the wall clock chimed 0900 and, on its final note, down came the decisive and authoritative gavel of senior court member, president and judge: Captain O'Brien. Surveying the room and noting still more onlookers, he nodded introspectively, finding the interest understandable as word of the culmination of this unusual case continued to circulate, promising an interruption in the boredom of daily routine.

They don't want to miss the final outcome, he thought to himself, and, come to think of it, if I were in their shoes, neither would I.

"The court will come to order! Everybody in their seats and quiet—now!

"When we adjourned yesterday, the defense counsel had concluded his interrogation of the accused—"

"Mr. President," broke in Trimble.

"Oh yes, Commander, I know: You concluded your interrogation but asked for the right of resumption if, after hearing the prosecution's interrogation, you deem it expedient. Is that it?"

"Right on, Sir," smiled Trimble. "I couldn't have stated it better."

Captain O'Brien returned a trace of a smile. "That's very compliant of you, Commander. Now, let us move on. Will the accused resume his place in the stand?"

Prompted by a nudge and motion from his counsel, Markowski did as directed.

The court president looked down at him. "Just a reminder to you, the accused: You are still under oath. Understand?"

"Yes, Sir—I do."

Captain O'Brien looked over at the prosecution table. "Commander Fields, at the conclusion of yesterday's session, you expressed a desire to interrogate the accused. Is that still your wish?"

"Most definitely. Sir."

"In that case, please proceed."

"Thank you, Mr. President." Fields turned and, again, focused those cold, stone-gray eyes on the accused for so long a time—seemingly endless to Markowski. Finally, he spoke.

"Markowski, you are accused of 'desertion from the Naval Service, the United States being in a state of war.' You understand that, don't you?"

"Y...yes, Sir."

"Do you agree with it?"

"Objection!" called Trimble. "The prosecution is treading old ground—and seemingly oblivious to what has transpired. If he needs a reminder, the plea was—and is—'not guilty.'"

"Yes, Commander, we agree that was the plea—followed immediately by a maudlin letter about his father in what appeared to be a convoluted attempt to justify it."

"Now we *strenuously* object!" exploded Trimble. "It's bad enough that the judge advocate calls our interrogation 'convoluted,' but he compounds it when he terms it 'maudlin.' It's an unforgivable term to apply to a survivor's account of the last days of a gallant Marine like Master Sergeant Matthew Markowski!"

Predictably, the crack of the gavel intervened. "Hold it right there—both of you!" instructed the president. "This bickering is getting entirely out of hand! I want you to get these interrogations back to a conventional basis. Do you understand?"

Trimble spoke first. "Yes, Sir, I do. Sorry, Mr. President."

His counterpart followed suit. "And I join in that, Sir. Now, if it pleases the court, I would like to ask the accused a question that might serve to mediate this controversy."

"Believe me, I sincerely hope you're right, Judge Advocate. Go ahead with your question."

Fields turned back to the accused. "I'm sorry if you feel I seemed to have maligned your father—certainly, that was not my intention. Rather, tell us, Markowski, do you believe desertion in time of war can *ever* be a justifiable action?"

"Objection again!" interjected Trimble. He turned to the court. "I firmly believe this controversy is caused by the fact that this case *is* an exception to the usual interpretation of 'desertion in time of war.'"

"Now, you have me baffled," said President O'Brien. "You are going to have to explain that statement, Counselor."

"Yes, Sir—and there is nothing I want to emphasize more. Now, we are getting down to the very essence of this case. I believe we can agree that the usual charge of 'desertion in time of war' is brought against one who leaves his post in order to *avoid* contact with the enemy— 'desertion in the face of the enemy,' if you will. This occurrence, however, is diametrically opposed to that. Fundamental to this case is the point that the accused left his post in order to *confront* the enemy *more* directly, *more* aggressively, *more* personally. Certainly, we are dealing with anything but a coward or malingerer here. Markowski did not leave his assigned post or 'desert in the face of the enemy'—call it what you will. No, not by any stretch of the imagination.

"In fact, he did the exact opposite: he left his post to *seek* and *destroy* the enemy, our military's mission in this war...and that is the very essence of this case."

"Interesting," mused President O'Brien. He turned to Fields. "I presume you have a response to that, Mr. Judge Advocate?"

"I most certainly do, Mr. President. If we begin to look for, make, and accept exceptions to the charge of desertion—exceptions based on individual interpretations of when or why it may be justified—the entire structure of Naval discipline will be shattered. The chain of command—and strict obedience to that command—becomes meaningless. It's the age-old mandate, gentlemen: 'Ours is not to question why—'"

"And the rest of that," broke in Trimble, "is: 'Ours is but to do or die'...and that's the whole point. *That* is *exactly* what the accused attempted."

Commander Fields' palm shot up. "No, that isn't quite correct, Counselor. That is the point that is being misinterpreted—misinterpreted most theatrically, I might add. If it's a matter of '*ours* is but to do or die,' that might be acceptable. That would be playing within the rules set by the group—in this case, the Navy itself. But, what we have here is something else—a personal interpretation that distorts those group rules. In effect, the accused has said, 'Forget the rules set by the group,' meaning the Navy. 'I will interpret them my way.' The distinction is *mine*, not *ours*."

The gavel resounded. "That's enough, gentlemen. We understand both of your points of view. Let the court be cleared."

— —

It was—and this time remained cleared for what seemed an interminable period to Markowski—giving him and his counsel an opportunity to quietly review their status.

"How do you feel about that session?" asked Commander Trimble. "Like it any better?"

"Oh, yes, Sir—I certainly did. Now I think we're winning, don't you?"

"Winning? No, lad, it's too early to tell. But, I grant you that it did serve to bring out our strongest points—ones that I had contemplated holding for a summation in mitigation. But, then, that's all right. It shouldn't do any harm—and, perhaps, it might even be *more* effective at this time. Anything else?"

"Yes, Sir, there is. If I have to answer that 'tough question'—the one about 'do you think that desertion is ever justified,' what should I tell them?"

"Knowing your story—your rationale—I don't have any worries about that. You've given that one plenty of thought, even before you did what you did. Just tell them the truth."

"But...but if I do and it gets me in trouble, they could give me the death penalty. Isn't that what you said?"

"Yes, that's what I said, and that is in the realm of possibility. But, it's nothing new; we've known that all along, haven't we? Look, young man, we've already pleaded guilty—to 'leaving your post,' but certainly not to 'desertion.' Just remember: 'desertion in the face of the enemy' is the bad one—and, certainly, that isn't what you did, is it?"

"No, Sir! I wouldn't do that, Sir."

"That's right. But when you did what you did, you had something in mind. What was it you attempted to do?"

"Well, Sir, I left the boat to try to find and kill the enemy."

"Correct, my boy. That's the truth, your honest story, and you must stick to it. And, look, you knew that 'leaving the boat' was a highly serious act—a departure from the norm—but you did it anyway. Isn't that right?"

Markowski nodded vigorously.

"It wasn't any spur of the moment decision, was it?"

Markowski shook his head indicating the negative this time.

"You thought about it a long time before you actually did it, didn't you?"

"Yes, Sir, that's right."

"But, Markowski, there's a weak point there. You say you thought about it for a long time, but you didn't know your boat was going to touch the beach itself near Lae until that very day, did you?"

"Ah...yes, Sir, that's right."

"How, then, do you equate that with the fact that you say you thought about it 'for a long time'?"

"I really did, Sir. But I thought, if things didn't change, I was going to do it at the first good opportunity."

"All right. If it comes up, just tell that story—the truth."

— —

The court reconvened. With the echo of his gavel, President O'Brien spoke. "The court is sorry for the length of that delay. It agrees this case is most unusual, but after considerable discussion, believes the judge advocate's query is not only valid, but properly delineates his appraisal of the issue. Accordingly, the defense counselor's objection to it is overruled. Now, Judge Advocate Fields, please restate your question."

Commander Fields nodded. "Thank you, Sir. The question we would like the accused to answer is this: Do you believe that, in time of war, desertion can ever be a justifiable action?"

After a prolonged silence, the president turned to Markowski. "Answer the question."

Markowski looked over to his counsel, who nodded his acquiescence.

The president looked sternly at Markowski. "Well, what is your answer?"

"Nor...normally no, but I think what I did was different."

"So your answer is 'yes'?"

185

"Yes, Sir, I guess it is."

Commander Fields turned in order to speak to Markowski, yet include the court as well.

"Might I summarize your answer by saying that, despite the fact you believe desertion is 'normally improper,' you believe it was an acceptable action in this instance because *you* decided it was?"

"Well, I..." Markowski glanced at Commander Trimble, who merely nodded again. "I guess...I guess that's right, Sir. I...I suppose I made a mistake."

Commander Fields, one hand on the witness railing, turned to the court and smiled.

President O'Brien asked, "Does that complete your interrogation, Judge Advocate?"

"It seems to, Sir. The prosecution could go on, but with this admission, it seems unnecessary. In our view, the accused has just pleaded guilty to knowingly and willfully appropriating government property to his own use, followed by desertion from his post and the Naval Service, the United States being in a state of war. On that, we'll rest."

"Thank you for your summation, Judge Advocate. Now, how about the defense counsel? Commander Trimble, you asked for an opportunity to probe the matter further at this point. Do you have anything more?"

Trimble rose to his feet. "Yes, Mr. President, I certainly do. Primarily, and with some possibility of reiteration, the defense would like to rephrase the so-called summary just made by the prosecution, on two counts.

"First, while the accused has pleaded guilty to appropriating arms and ammunition intended for the Allied Service, the phrase 'to his own use' is a misnomer. In taking the property, he intended—and succeeded—in

186

using it against the common enemy. This, gentlemen, is not 'his' war...it is 'our' war: the declared war of the United States and its allies.

"Second, the accusation of the judge advocate that this appropriation of weaponry was 'followed by desertion from his post and the Naval Service' summarizes and highlights the cardinal point—one I've made before, but it seems evident that a repetitive rebuttal is called for. In that vein, I wish to reiterate the point that, normally such desertion implies—at the minimum—that this is done 'in the face of the enemy.' In this case, however, the cardinal point is that Markowski's action was its very antithesis. If it *is* desertion, it is desertion in order to *search out and destroy the enemy.* That, gentlemen of the court, is the crux of the case. The difference is significant—and crystal clear."

A seemingly irate Commander Fields bounced to his feet. "Objection, Mr. President—a *strenuous* one. The counselor is right when he states he would like to cover what he calls 'the cardinal point' again. The point *has* been made before, considered by the defendant himself—and self-described as 'a mistake.'"

"Objection sustained." The president peered down at the counsel for the defense.

"Anything else, Commander?"

"No, Sir. The defense has stated its case—and rests."

Captain O'Brien turned to Fields. "And you, Judge Advocate, are you finished?"

Commander Fields, looking pleased, stated, "Yes, Sir, we, too, rest."

President O'Brien looked from judge advocate to counsel.

"In the eyes of this court, you gentlemen are both to be commended for conducting your assignments admirably. Now, the court declares this hearing complete and will recess to ponder its verdict. Pending such verdict, the accused will be returned to the brig."

The crack of the gavel punctuated the final note.

— —

Commander Trimble and Markowski sat at the small desk in the now familiar, stark, and equally small brig office, the distraught and dejected-appearing prisoner with head in hands. Finally, he looked up.

"Commander—Sir, what do you think their decision will be?"

"Just what do you mean by that?"

"Do you think I have any chance of getting off?"

"Good Lord, young man, you can't still be hoping they'll find you innocent! You're accused of desertion in time of war. Call it 'slipped off the boat,' or any other verbalism, but that's what you did. We've pleaded not guilty, to the charge of desertion in the hope that the fact you carried the war *to* the enemy will encourage them to reduce it to something less—like absence without leave. But that's the very best we can hope for. That decision is up to them—plus whatever punishment they choose to recommend."

"What do you think that might be, Sir?"

"As you already know—and we've gone over this time and time again—if they find you guilty of desertion, it could be anything up to that extreme one: death."

"Oh my God...I thought that was over! After all this, they wouldn't do that, would they, Sir?"

"*Again*, lad, 'wouldn't' I don't know. I certainly hope not—but you must understand, they *could*. As I've told you before, desertion is near the top of the list of the worst crimes listed in Rocks and Shoals*. Our only hope is what I expressed in my closing remarks, that because of your youth, your feelings for your father, his distinguished record, plus the cardinal point that you didn't do what you did to avoid combat, but to seek it—well, they just might be lenient."

"But, do *you* think they might, Sir?"

"Look, Markowski, let's be realistic. Like Commander Fields said, you can't expect them to take pity on every guy who takes military law into his own hands and twists it just because he thinks he has a special reason to do so. Let's knock off this speculation now. As I've told you before: Prepare for the worst, and pray for the best. I'm with you in that."

"But, but—"

"No more 'buts.' It isn't doing any good. It's back in the brig with you now until the court reaches its decision."

Trimble rose to leave, signaled the guard, then turned back.

"By the way, young man...good luck."

* Naval Courts and Boards, 1937 version.

20

Hours crept by—hours ever more tortured for Markowski. With the brig constructed as an inner compartment, there was nothing to see or do but try to read—and reread without comprehending—the few old and well-thumbed magazines while pondering and repondering the proceedings of the court and apprehensively speculating on the outcome.

Finally, late in the afternoon, Commander Trimble reappeared.

"Young man, I have news for you, news of a sort. The court has sent word that they have reached a decision. No, we don't know what that is, and President O'Brien has judged it too late in the day to reconvene. Accordingly, he has set a time of 0900 tomorrow morning."

Markowski groaned. "Tomorrow morning? We have to wait *that* long?"

Lord, the poor kid looks awful, thought Trimble. He must be going through the tortures of the damned—and who can blame him?

"Yes, that's right. There is nothing we can do but go along with the president's decision. And no, we don't have a clue as to what the judgment is. Just try to get a good night's sleep—and I will see you at court in the morning."

"But...but, Sir, isn't there some indication of their decision?"

"No, but if it took this long for them to reach an agreement, I would guess there very likely wasn't any unanimity of opinion."

"No una...unanimity? Is that good or bad?"

"Look, young man, I don't know for sure, but my hunch would be that a quick response would probably have spelled bad tidings for us. Think of it in that light while you try to get some rest. And, again, if I were you, I wouldn't forget those prayers. I'll join you in that. Good night, lad."

— —

As 0900 neared, the courtroom began to fill. Although restricted solely to carefully screened military personnel, it seemed a surprisingly large group to Trimble—undoubtedly a further indication of the interest kindled as word of the impending denouement of the unusual case was bandied about the base.

A Marine MP led Markowski out of the brig, ashore, and into the courtroom. One glance sufficed for Trimble to realize that a good night's rest had again eluded his charge. Exhausted, pale, obviously heavily laden with anxiety, the poor fellow appeared near the end of his tether.

Trimble patted the adjoining chair. "Sit down, Markowski—and try to relax."

"That's easy for you to say, Sir."

"No, it's not. Believe me, lad, I'm with you in this. I agree, it's not easy at all—but our time has come."

The clock rang nine bells, and with it came the accompanying crack of Judge O'Brien's gavel.

"The court will come to order!" To a large degree, it did.

"I wish to announce the decision of the court in this case of the United States versus Motor Machinist's Mate Third Class Myron Markowski.

"But first, allow me to state—particularly for the edification of the new spectators in this room—that reaching a decision in this uncommon case was far from easy. Oh, there was no question of the guilt of the accused— except for whether it should be of desertion in time of war as charged, or of a lesser imputation as suggested by the defense. Initially, no unanimity prevailed on that point. In the end, however, the former prevailed: guilty—guilty of desertion, the United States being in a state of war."

"Oh!" gasped Markowski as if stabbed.

Trimble gripped his charge's arm. "Shhhh-hold on."

President O'Brien continued. "It was the degree of retribution that became the main problem for the court. At the outset there was a deep division of opinion—with a seemingly adamant minority claiming that 'if the punishment were to fit the crime,' a possible sentence of 'death' could be contemplated. In the end, however, the majority's acceptance of, and sincere appreciation with, the circumstances that led the accused to take the war into his own hands prevailed, resulting in a moderation of the potential recommended penalty."

Defense Counsel Trimble gave his charge a sharp nudge. "We're over the major hurdle," came the glowing whisper.

The president of the court continued. "As I have indicated, there was unanimity insofar as the charge of 'desertion in time of war' is concerned. It was the collateral element—'desertion with intent to avoid hazardous duty'—that became the stumbling block for the minority point of view. Clearly—as was so well elucidated by the counsel for the defense—this component was not only not applicable in this case, but its very antithesis was extant. Extraordinary measures were taken by the accused to—if I may use the word—to *commit* the opposite: carry his own war *to* the enemy, faulty as his reasoning may have been. That, in conjunction with the minor, but prevalent point of his youth, plus the aforementioned matter of his understandable, though inordinate, reaction to the grievous death of his distinguished father at the hands of the enemy, prompted the majority of the court to insist on an abated punishment."

"That's good, isn't it, Sir?" whispered Markowski

Trimble held up a hand in a cautionary gesture. "Wait, son—wait!"

"On the other hand," continued the president, "two negative factors contributed to our final judgment. First was the endangerment to our vital allies, the coastwatchers, posed by Markowski's persistent actions. Second was the fact that the termination of his campaign was anything but voluntary, having only been effected by his apprehension and arrest.

"Accordingly, and with all that in mind,"...a complete hush fell over the courtroom..."we sentence the accused, Motor Machinist's Mate Third Class Myron Markowski, to a dishonorable discharge, forfeiture of all pay, and confinement for three years."

Disorder supplanted the silence, an immediate covering of babble blanketing the area only to be slowly subdued by the rhythmic beat of the president's fatigued gavel. "This court is not finished! It will come to order—and stay in order!" Slowly, it did.

"Now," continued President O'Brien looking with curiosity at the defense desk, "does the counsel for the accused have anything to add?"

"Yes, Sir, I do. If it please the court, I would like to speak in mitigation."

"The court understands—and is hardly surprised. Go right ahead, Counselor."

Commander Trimble moved to a more effective position for addressing all present: the court and onlookers.

"Gentlemen, the defense accepts—with some measure of disappointment and reluctance—the verdict and recommended punishment assigned by this court. Nevertheless, knowing that this testimony and verdict are destined for review and evaluation by the Convening Authority, there are certain facets that deserve to be emphasized—and others that should be added—before a full and fair evaluation can be portrayed.

"Initially, we urge that an objective view of the defendent, Myron Markowski, be taken. Here is a young man—younger than eighteen at time of enlistment, and not much over it now—who volunteered for motor torpedo boats in order to avenge the death of his revered father, Master Sergeant Matthew Markowski, a gallant and highly respected career Marine and one of the first to give his life in this current war.

"Frustrated with his assignment to seclusion in the engine room of a PT boat during combat, and in order to achieve his dream of a more personalized vengeance, the son—mistakenly by his own admission in retrospect—armed himself and 'left the boat' in order to seek out and destroy our common enemy.

"In the course of his campaign, he inadvertently made the further judgmental error of occasionally seeking aid and comfort from Coastwatchers Donegal and Jollymore, whom he considered to be compatriots in his war against the Japanese. Although they protested strongly, he—the accused—mistakenly continued to seek them out. I would like to point out and stress that, fortunately, neither of these valiant gentlemen or their program, seems to have been harmed by these actions.

"Further, the prosecution has attributed the wounding of Ensign Stringer to the actions of the accused. We, however, would like to underscore the fact that this unfortunate incident occurred well *after* Markowski had left the scene. The ill-fated patrol in question was made at the behest of Captain Mooney—commodore of PT's Southwest Pacific—in order to obtain a deposition that, in hindsight, seems redundant, since Mr. Donegal was, and is, on hand to authoritively describe the actions of the accused when needed.

"Finally, I would like to reiterate the response of the accused when PT 143 was attacked by Japanese aircraft on its trip down to the rear base at Kana Kopa in Milne Bay. Despite the fact that he was a prisoner and not a regular member of the crew, he willingly—nay, eagerly—took a position at the smoke generator—a battle station that proved vital in the subsequent engagement—and, quoting the captain of the PT in question, 'did an excellent job of it.'"

Court President O'Brien looked down at Trimble. "That's it, Commander? Anything more?"

"If it please the court, only this: It's true a mistake was made—a mistake retrospectively and remorsefully admitted to by the accused, a young, manifestly inexperienced, misguided, but unusually courageous, son of a distinguished father. Clearly, it behooves the Naval Service to regard this as a life and career to be redirected and utilized—certainly not one to be incarcerated when our country is seeking young men of such displayed determination and patriotism." Trimble turned to the bench. "And that, Mr. President, completes my remarks in mitigation."

Captain O'Brien motioned towards the prosecution. "And you, Commander Fields? Do you have anything you would like to add?"

"Nothing of great weight, Mr. President, but it seems the only point that we haven't properly rebutted is the defense counselor's consistent and assertive portrayal of the accused as 'unusually young.' That, we must admit—but his lying about his age in order to enter the service prematurely is his own doing. *He* is the one who made that judgment—a judgment that put him into the same category as the thousands of other young men only a few months or days older. Certainly, we shouldn't suggest the precedent that these thousands should be excused from compliance with the Articles for the Government of the Navy simply because of their age—and in this case, to reiterate—an age falsely concealed by his own willful prevarification. And, with that, Mr. President and gentlemen of the court, we rest our answer to my talented counterpart's remarks in mitigation."

President O'Brien looked from Fields to Trimble and smiled. "Speaking of reiteration, I would like to emphasize my previous remark that, in the eyes of this court, you two gentlemen are both to be commended for conducting your assignments admirably.

"Now, let a record of this trial be prepared, authenticated, and forwarded to the Convening Authority. This case will be adjourned and suspended pending that review and, in the interim, the accused is to be returned to confinement."

The gavel sounded a culminating whack. "So be it."

— —

Markowski and his defense counsel resumed their seats in the room adjoining the brig. Lieutenant Commander Trimble took the measure of his charge: feet tightly crossed, hands continually wrung, face skewed tightly — near tears perhaps? All in all, a thoroughly wretched sight. Trimble reached over and touched his charge's knee. Markowski jumped as if shocked.

"Wha...what is it, Sir?"

"Easy, son. I just wanted to congratulate you."

"Congratulate me! What for?"

"For avoiding that death sentence—or life imprisonment. That's 'what for.'"

"But, Sir—three years! That's almost a lifetime!"

"Oh come now, Markowski. That's a typical young man's view. I want to remind you that it could have been a great deal worse. And, if it comes to that, after three years, what'll you be—twenty one? And, don't forget, it's still not over."

"What do you mean, Sir?"

"Just that. Didn't you hear the president of the court say the case is only adjourned? This is different than civil law. Under Naval Law, it now goes to the Convening Authority—the Admiral for his review and subsequent approval, disapproval, or modification. That was the whole point of my summary in mitigation; it was strictly for the Admiral's eyes and ears."

"But, Sir, do you really think the Admiral will do that?"

"You bet—in theory at least. But, as I've told you before, in practice it will be his legal staff who will do it. You must understand that, until it is reviewed and affirmed or modified, your case remains open—wide open. It's not finished," his counsel grinned, "and, my boy, neither are you."

"All right, Sir. I think I understand. Now what do I do?"

"You just crawl right back in that brig of yours and wait—wait until you hear from me again. And remember, I'm still on your side, and if there's anything you need or want that you can't get here, ask them to give me a call."

"Thank you, Sir. And Commander, thanks for everything."

21

Time crept by for Markowski—limped along. The week-long days were impossible to fill. He attempted a letter to his mother, but after reviewing the disjointed, inconclusive result, tore it up in frustration. Surely she would gain no joy in reading that!

Out of desperation, he turned back to all the faded books and dog-eared magazines he could get his hands on—including those Commander Trimble had sent down—finding them easy to read, but impossible to assimilate.

Staying awake seemed improbable, but attempting to sleep proved worse. The tedious passage of time was spent in a fragmented, desultory limbo around the cyclical theme: "Kicked out of the Navy...loss of pay...three years in the stir...Oh, my God!"

— —

Meanwhile, at Seventh Fleet Headquarters in a mundane, brick office building in downtown Brisbane, three members of Admiral Woodstock's JAG staff were deeply involved in a review of recent incidents, cases, findings, and recommendations. All was proceeding in routine fashion until one—a Lieutenant Commander Ralph Coffey—looked up from the sheaf of papers on his desk.

"Fellows, have either of you had a chance to read the minutes of the case involving a motormac third class by the name of Markowski?"

"I certainly have," replied Brady, one of the two lieutenants at nearby desks. He reached for a set of papers separated from the stack of more routine matters of the day. "Here it is...all by its lonesome!"

"Well, isn't that a coincidence," chimed in the remaining member—a Lieutenant McCarthy. "I've just been scratching my head over the same one. I've never seen or heard of a case like it. Frankly, I don't know what to recommend."

"And you, Brady, what is your opinion?"

"I'm inclined to go along with the recommendation of the court...but, still—like friend McCarthy here—some facets of it bother me."

"Like what?"

"More than one—but the main stumbling block for me is the fact that this fellow Markowski wanted to carry his vengeance *to* the enemy, not run *from* them. He's anything but a coward."

"You mean it's a kind of a 'like father, like son' situation, don't you?"

"In part, yes—but, in another part, no."

"Well, well," grinned senior member Coffey, "you characters aren't being very helpful. I was hoping you would have more positive convictions regarding this case than I do, but obviously you don't—which makes it three strikes and out."

"Tell me, Ralph," said Brady, "I understand the three strikes—but what's the 'out'?"

"Why, out of the door and out of our hands. Much as I hate to do it to the Old Man, I believe we should admit our quandary and submit this material and its summary to the Admiral. Any objections?"

"No Sir," came the concerted reply.

"All right, my equally indecisive cohorts, here it goes," said the lieutenant commander reaching for and pressing the button under his desk. The door swung open and a yeoman appeared.

"Casey, take this material on the Markowski case to Admiral Woodstock's office and tell his yeoman the legal staff apologizes to the Admiral for the intrusion, but it is stalemated on a most unusual case and requests his guidance."

— —

It was midmorning the following day when the telephone shattered the silence in the JAG office-and Yeoman Casey burst through Lieutenant Commander Coffey's door without knocking.

"Sir, it's Admiral Woodstock for you!"

"Really?" said Coffey, sitting up straight in his chair as he reached for the phone. "Good morning, Admiral. Coffey here."

"Coffey," came the reply, "I've just gone over the Markowski case, and all I can say is: '"I'll be damned!"'"

Coffey grinned into the phone. "And that, Sir, is the very same conclusion we came to."

"Well...ahem...I do have some thoughts on the matter and want to see you—along with this fellow, Markowski."

"You want me to bring him to your office? Yes, Sir, will do, but I'll have to dig him out of the brig of that ship down at the dock. That will take a little time."

"Well 'dig him out' as you put it, and have him here — let's make it at 1400 today. That'll give him a change of venue from that brig. And, by the way, have those two counsels, Lieutenant Commanders Trimble and Fields, with you if possible."

"Aye aye, Admiral. I'll get right on it."

— —

The door to the brig opened and Lieutenant Commander Trimble knocked on the prisoner's cell.

"Markowski—get out of that sack, comb your hair, and put on a fresh uniform. We're going to town to see the Admiral!"

"The Admiral!" gasped Markowski. "We...*me*?"

"Yes, we—you and me. Now, get with it. You don't keep an admiral waiting—particularly this one!"

— —

The four—Lieutenant Commanders Fields, Trimble, and Coffey and their overawed and disconcerted prisoner saluted their way into the well-guarded, ex-office building in central Brisbane, now housing the headquarters of General MacArthur and his staff, including those of the Navy's Seventh Fleet. After identifying themselves to the Admiral's yeoman, the group took seats in the reception area.

Shortly thereafter, a two-star Marine Corps general entered, nodded to the officers, paused momentarily in an obvious appraisal of the accused, then went directly into the Admiral's office. Norman Trimble noted the change it caused in Markowski: What had been his pale, squirming, highly distraught charge was now in his chair, eyes rounded, mouth agape in astonishment.

After another delay—a half an hour at the most—the yeoman's desk came to life as a deep, amplified voice directed: "Send in the three officers and the prisoner."

The office they entered was surprisingly stark for its importance: the desk large, the carpeting deep but plain, the six surrounding chairs identical but nondescript, and an open conference room in an ell to the side—all brought to life by a large American flag, the three-star burgee of a vice-admiral and, most of all, the presence of Admiral Woodstock and the Marine major-general.

The Admiral himself was awesomely impressive to Markowski, and looked the way an admiral should look in his estimation: well-tanned, with thick greying hair, clad in crisp khakis accented by the gold, three-star epaulets of a vice-admiral and a colorful array of service ribbons from breast pocket to shoulder board.

"Greetings gentlemen," said the Admiral to the three officers and acknowledged Markowski with a nod, then a piercing scrutiny. "This, by the way, is the senior Marine on my staff: General Tremaine.

"I have been briefed on this case in which you JAG officers have been involved, and I agree that it is unique in several respects—unique enough to compel me to probe a bit further.

"First, let me start where I understand the incident itself began—with that father of yours, Markowski. I have talked to General Tremaine here, and find that he not only knows of Master Sergeant Matthew Markowski, but he knew him personally. Tell us about him, General."

The General chiefly directed his words at the prisoner. "Markowski, I understand you thought the world of your father—and, in my opinion, you are absolutely right in doing so. He—Master Sergeant Matt Markowski—was everything a career Marine is supposed to be: proud, strong, aggressive, but—now, mark my words, young man—*he played by the rules.* Do you understand what I'm getting at?"

"Yes, Sir, I...I believe I do."

"Your father served with me on two different occasions, and I always knew I could count on him to do his assigned job extremely well—correctly and dependably. You have every right to be proud of him."

The seated Markowski seemed to grow taller. "Thank you, Sir. I am."

The Admiral broke in. "Markowski, we understand you wanted to be a Marine, but failing that, joined the Navy and applied for PT boats?"

"Y...Yes, Sir," said an obviously nervous Markowski.

"And just why did you do that?"

"Well...mostly, Sir, because of what they—the Japanese—did to my dad."

"You wanted revenge?"

"Yes, Sir. That...that's right."

"So, as I understand it, you stole a gun and ammunition and started your own war—took on the whole Japanese army yourself?"

"I—well not the 'whole' thing—but, sort of...I'm afraid that's right, Sir."

The Admiral continued to study the prisoner. Then, he continued, "Tell me, young man, would you like to be like your father?"

"Oh, *yes, sir*, I certainly would."

Admiral Woodstock nodded. "Did you hear what General Tremaine said about that father of yours?"

"Yes, Sir, I did."

"Did you hear him describe him as 'proud, strong and aggressive'?"

Markowski came forward in his chair. "Yes, Sir, I did."

"And you say you would like to be like him?"

"Oh, yes, Sir."

"General Tremaine also had something else to say about him—that father of yours: 'He always did his job correctly and dependably.' Did you hear that?"

"Ah...yes, Sir, I did."

"Doesn't that spell out the difference between you and that father of yours?"

"Yes, Sir. I...I made a bad mistake...I wish I hadn't done it that way."

Commander Trimble raised a hand. "May I interject a word here, Admiral?" The Admiral nodded. "I've spent a great deal of time with this young man, and I'd like to add my conviction that he is being absolutely sincere in this...this apology. Blame it on youth, immaturity, lack of experience, and the need for guidance, but I firmly believe he is honestly contrite over what he did. Not so much *what* he did, but the *way* he did it."

The Admiral turned to Commander Fields. "And what is your opinion, Commander?"

"I agree with my adversary," he smiled, "and friend, Commander Trimble. And, judging by the decision—or lack of it—of the reviewers in sending this to you, I am quite sure I speak for them as well. The balance to that opinion, however, is: Does that *excuse* this young man's conduct?"

Admiral Woodstock took it from there. He pointed at the prisoner. "Markowski, would you still like to avenge your father's treatment at the hands of the Japanese?"

205

"Oh, *yes, Sir,* I would!"

"I mean the right way...within the rules?"

There was a thoughtful pause. "Yes, Sir, I sure would."

"Then," said the Admiral with a hint of a smile, "tell me, Markowski—can you swim?"

In the midst of the obviously astonished group, Markowski—easily the most dumfounded of all-managed a "Wha...what, Sir?"

"Can you swim—swim well, that is?"

"Oh yes, Sir—I like it. I'm good at it, Sir."

"I suppose," smiled the Admiral, "and I wouldn't be at all surprised that you're all wondering what I'm getting at."

Lieutenant Commander Coffey grinned. "If I may be so bold, I believe I can reply for the group with a resounding '*yes, Sir!*'"

"And I don't blame you," said the Admiral. "Let me begin with the intelligence that our recent landing on Tarawa resulted in a horrendous number of personnel losses—approximately 20 percent—due to the unexpected grounding of tanks and landing craft short of the beach—exposing the troops to an inordinate amount of murderous fire from the enemy. In response, Admiral Kelly Turner, commander of our amphibious forces, has ordered the immediate creation of special teams to surreptitiously precede future landing forces in order to ascertain the extent of natural and man-made obstacles, thereby guiding our troops in more safely.

"Now, Markowski, I'm told you are aggressive—wanted to go in with the Marines, as a matter of fact. Correct?"

"Y...Yes, Sir, that's true."

"Well, then, how would you like an opportunity to join these new special forces and train to not only go in with the Marines, but go in *ahead* of them?"

Markowski's face glowed. "I'd like that very much, Sir!"

"This is a volunteer group. Do you choose to join them?"

"Oh, *yes, Sir!*"

"Then, these will be your orders: You will be sent to Fort Pierce, Florida, to train with these newly created Underwater Demolition Teams*. However—and listen very carefully—with it will go the proviso that you are to strictly adhere to their rules and regulations of appropriate conduct and, if you violate them in any way, the punishment assigned you by the recent Court will be regenerated and you will be penalized as recommended. Do you understand?"

"Yes, Sir—I do."

"And you accept these terms in their entirety?"

"Yes, Sir—I do."

"And you are now volunteering for Underwater Demolition Team training?"

"Yes, Sir—I sure am."

"Do you have any comments?"

"Just 'thank you,' Sir. Thank you very much!"

"There's only one way to thank me, young man: get out of here now, *and just go out and prove yourself!*"

---

* Forerunner of the justifiably renowned Navy SEALS.

Order Form

QTY.	Title	Price	Can. Price	Total
	Recompense **- Russ Hamachek**	**$14.95**	**$19.95** **CN**	
	Shipping and Handling Add $3.50 for orders in the US/Add $7.50 for Global Priority			
	Sales tax (WA state residents only, add 8.9%)			
	Total enclosed			

Telephone Orders:
Call **1-800-461-1931**
Have your VISA or
MasterCard ready.

INTL. Telephone Orders:
Toll free **1-877-250-5500**
Have your credit card ready.

Fax Orders:
425-398-1380
Fill out this order form and fax.

Postal Orders:
Hara Publishing
P.O. Box 19732
Seattle, WA 98109

E-mail Orders:
harapub@foxinternet.net

Method of Payment:

☐ Check or Money Order

☐ *VISA*

☐ MasterCard

Expiration Date: _____

Card #: _____

Signature: _____

Name _____
Address _____
City _____ **State** ___ **Zip** _____
Phone (   ) _____ Fax (   ) _____

Quantity discounts are available.
Call **425-398-3679** for more information.
Thank you for your order!

209